Puffin Books

ME AND MY MI

At first Ringo only ... ... when his brother ... ... would they? ... ... ome all the way to ... ... to have a look, so Ringo decid... it was ...vis took him out for a hamburger and ... ...Like to do a little job for us?' Ringo knew what sort of job it was going to be.

Delivering a laundry bag to a laundrette *seemed* simple enough. But it meant catching a bus, and Ringo wasn't too strong on reading words and figures. He was quite likely to get a number 41 muddled with 14 – and that was how he came to find himself in the wrong laundrette, late at night, with a million pounds' worth of laundry and only 2p in his pocket. It was the start of a series of wild adventures, which were to lead through a derelict fire station, a rich businessman's office, the hideout of a mysterious gang, and a narrowboat on the Regent's Park Canal. Other people were after that million too – some of them for very unpleasant reasons – and it was a hard task for a small boy who couldn't read, on his own in a strange part of London, to keep himself and the picture safe. How he managed makes very exciting, and often hilarious, reading.

Clive King was born in Richmond, Surrey in 1924. He was the second in a family of four sons. The family moved to a village in Kent when he was small, and this later became the setting for *Stig of the Dump*. He got an open exhibition to Downing College, Cambridge. During the war he served in the RNVR and later, after completing his studies, he joined the British Council. He now lives in a converted marshman's cottage in Norfolk, which is full of his own creations, such as a homemade built-in ironing board. He has three children and five grandchildren.

BAR CODE
NEXT PAGE

Other books by Clive King

STIG OF THE DUMP
THE TOWN THAT WENT SOUTH
THE TWENTY-TWO LETTERS
THE SOUND OF PROPELLERS

ME AND MY MILLION

CLIVE KING

PUFFIN BOOKS

PUFFIN BOOKS

Published by the Penguin Group
Penguin Books Ltd, 27 Wrights Lane, London W8 5TZ, England
Penguin Books USA Inc., 375 Hudson Street, New York, New York 10014, USA
Penguin Books Australia Ltd, Ringwood, Victoria, Australia
Penguin Books Canada Ltd, 10 Alcorn Avenue, Toronto, Ontario, Canada M4V 3B2
Penguin Books (NZ) Ltd, 182–190 Wairau Road, Auckland 10, New Zealand

Penguin Books Ltd, Registered Offices: Harmondsworth, Middlesex, England

First published by Kestrel Books 1976
Published in Puffin Books 1979
20 19 18 17 16 15 14 13

Copyright © Clive King, 1976
All rights reserved

Printed in England by Clays Ltd, St Ives plc
Set in Linotype Pilgrim

to the Pirate Club

CONTENTS

1·MILLION-POUND PICTURE

My brother Elvis says, 'Come on, we're going for a walk!'

I said, 'Me, go for a walk?'

'Go to school then,' he says.

I knew he was joking. We got on a twenty-four bus, then we got off and started walking. There's this hill, in London. At the bottom there are old men playing games with these big black wooden balls. There are some little kids shut up in a playground, and some posh people in white clothes hitting tennis balls. But I don't think they're very good at it.

Then there's a lot of grass with dogs running about on it, and the people who have the dogs shouting at them to come here. There's a pond with people sitting behind fishing rods. I talked to this young kid, sitting looking at his line going down into the water.

'Ever catch anything?' I asked him.

'Got a big'un last year,' he says. 'Mostly they get away, though.'

I suppose it's all right, when all of a sudden there's a fish come from nowhere under the dirty water and hooked on to your line. And you can do what you like with it, fry it with chips if you like. Costs you nothing, except a lot of waiting around. Me, I could never find the time for it.

There's another pond with people *swimming* in it. They looked cold.

'Do they get prizes for it or something?' I asked Elvis. He

9

said they sometimes got their picture in the papers if it was very cold. Didn't seem worth it.

Another pond. People playing with little boats that go by radio.

I said to Elvis, 'Here, how about making one that fires rockets? Or torpedoes! And sink all the other boats!' I got a dirty look from one of the blokes standing in the water in big boots. They're not kids that play with these boats, you know. Must cost a packet, all that radio gear. Can't let the kids get their hands on them!

Like the people flying the kites. It was mostly grownups. All right, some of them were dads, letting the kids have a go on the end of the string. But there were old old blokes, holding their strings and looking up at their kites stuck up there in the sky, proud as if they were jet pilots.

We walked on, up and up, and it was all trees and grass, and a few guys and girls lying around. My new shoes were killing me. They were ones with big thick wooden soles. Everybody was wearing them then – especially half-pint sized blokes like me. But you don't reckon to *walk* in them.

'Can we go home now?' I said to Elvis.

'We're not there yet,' he says.

'Where's there?' I asked him. 'The North freezin' Pole?'

'Come on!' he says. 'We're not doing this for fun.'

That was all right then. I was beginning to wonder.

There were more big old trees with paths underneath them. I stopped and said, 'Look! Look at that!'

There was an animal running around loose in the middle of the path. It wasn't a cat or a dog.

'You're not scared of a squirrel, are you?' Elvis asked. He was laughing at me. Of course I wasn't scared. I picked up a stick and chucked it at the squirrel, but it missed and the squirrel ran up a tree.

We came out of the wood and saw the house on the top of the hill. It was just a big house with a lot of windows.

'That's it,' says Elvis.

'Oh?' I said. 'Can we go home now?'

'We're going in,' he says.

'I didn't know you had rich friends,' I said.

Well, Elvis, he's only half my brother really. So he's half at home and half somewhere else. He's old, more than twenty. They gave him this soppy name after some old pop star. I don't know, maybe he did have rich friends.

'Nit!' says Elvis. 'Anyone can go in.'

So in we go. There are these old men in blue suits with letters on them, words maybe. They look at you like they're saying to themselves, 'Here comes trouble!' It's because of Elvis, he has these studs on his clothes.

It's a big old house with big shiny floors and big windows you can see the trees and grass through. I still couldn't see what we'd come all this way for. There's nothing happening except people mooching round. You know, like there's a family, mum and dad and the kids, and they've got a car, and Dad says, 'It's coming on to rain, let's go and look at this old house.'

The only things to look at are these pictures hanging on the walls. They've got gold frames round them, but I don't think real gold. There's glass in front of them and they're all about the olden days with people wearing a lot of old clothes or no clothes at all.

Once I started looking at them I could see there were things happening in some of them, like soldiers fighting or ships fighting. But quite a lot of them were only places, or trees and grass. There were even pictures of old cows!

I could see through the window of the house there were people buying ices and drinks at a stall, so I said to Elvis, 'What about a coke or something?'

But he was standing in front of a picture saying to himself, 'A million pounds!' I said I only wanted ten pee for a drink.

'That picture,' he says. 'It's worth a million pounds.'

Of course he had to be joking, but I asked, 'Does it say so on the ticket?' All the pictures had these tickets with words and figures on them.

'I read about it,' he says. He reads a lot, my brother, news-papers and magazines and that. Comes easy to him. He even believes what he reads.

I turned to an old bloke in a blue suit standing near the picture and said, 'Hey, mister, is this picture worth a million pounds?'

He gives me a sour look, like telling me to keep my dirty mitts off it. 'You might put it like that,' he says. 'It's priceless.'

I remember my uncle saying he didn't know anything that hadn't got a price. I said to Elvis, 'Can't be worth all that much. Or they wouldn't leave it hanging on the wall, would they?'

I went up to it to feel it, to see if the frame *was* solid gold perhaps. But all of a sudden the bloke in the blue suit was in my way, standing between me and the picture.

He looked down at me. 'What d'you think I'm standing here all day for?' he asks, quiet but a bit narked.

He wasn't all that old, this bloke. Fat, but more like one of these wrestlers. I got back.

'I bet you know all about karate, kung fu and that, eh mister?' I said to him. He didn't say yes or no, just smiled a bit.

'Do you stand there all night and all?' I asked him. He sniffed, but he didn't really seem to mind me chatting him up. Made a change from seeing people gawping at the old pictures, I suppose.

'If you're thinking of lifting it after dark,' he says, 'You'd have a surprise or two.'

I looked at the big old windows. No bars or anything. I could get through those quick enough! I nearly said so, but – well, he might think I knew too much about it.

'You might get in,' he says, like he could see what I was thinking. 'But it wouldn't take us long to know you were there.'

'You got dogs then?' I asked.

And he says, 'What, lifting their legs against all this priceless furniture?' There were some old chairs standing about. Looked like the moths had got at them.

I said, 'I bet you've got invisible eyes, bugs, the lot.' He didn't say anything. But I looked round the big room and thought maybe it wasn't such a crummy old joint after all. Had secret panels and trapdoors and all, I shouldn't wonder.

Another blue suit comes mooching across the floor towards us, and my bloke shuts up, like he's said too much already.

At the same time Elvis calls to me across the room, 'I say, Ringo, do come and look at this little painting!'

Ringo, that's what they call me. I think it was some other old pop star my mum liked. Sometimes they call me Bingo too. I don't like that one either.

I went over to Elvis to see what had got into him, talking like the other wet-looking people there. He was standing in front of a picture of a horse.

'It's all right,' I said. 'Except they've gone and cut its tail off. You going to put some money on it?'

'That horse died a hundred years ago, like everything else here,' he says. 'I'm looking at the window.'

'Looking out the window?' I said. He didn't need my help to look at trees and grass.

'Looking *at* the window,' he says, very quiet.

Oy, oy, I thought. He's an expert on windows, Elvis is. Not cleaning them, you know. Getting through them.

And he says, 'Wouldn't you like to have a coke *and* an ice cream? You done all right, kid. I couldn't have asked all them questions myself. But don't *over*do it, see?'

We went out and he bought me a coke and a heart on a stick. He's funny, my brother, but he's all right sometimes.

We stood in the road outside and I sucked my lolly.

'What are we waiting for?' I asked.

'A two one O,' says Elvis.

'You mean there's a bus right outside the door?' I said. 'We needn't have walked all that way?'

'Belt up, kid,' he says. 'You've had a coke and a lolly and you've nearly touched a million-pound picture. Worth a bit of a walk, ain't it?'

Well, I couldn't say it wasn't. I thought a lot about that picture the next few days. I even went to school so I could tell

13

my pals about this million-pound picture. But I didn't tell them. You know, I didn't think I was finished with it.

It didn't surprise me when Elvis came and took me out to a caf and gave me hamburger and chips. Shane was with us. Shane's Elvis's mate.

'Like to do a little job for us?' Elvis says to me. *Here it comes*, I thought.

'I still think you're crazy,' says Shane, like they'd been arguing about this before.

'All you got to do is carry this laundry bag to a laundrette,' says Elvis to me.

I didn't go much on *that* job! 'That's a girl's job,' I said.

'You'll do,' says Elvis. 'Call yourself Little Ringlets if you like.' He kept his legs out of the way under the table, or I'd have got at them with my wooden soles.

'Look,' says Shane to Elvis. 'You don't let a little kid like that loose in London with a –'

'That's it, ain't it?' Elvis didn't let him finish. 'No one else would. That's why it's going to work, see?'

There was more in this laundry bag than old socks, I thought. I'd go along with it.

'Do I have to walk and all?' I asked Elvis.

'Just take a couple of buses,' he says. 'A two one O and a forty-one.'

Two one O, that told me something. That was the one that went past the big house.

'I'll give you the fare,' says Elvis.

'Big deal!' I said. 'What about a few ten pees for the washing machines?'

'Never mind the washing,' says Elvis. 'There'll be a girl called Marilyn at the laundrette. You just hand the bag over to her. And maybe she'll give you another lolly on a stick.'

Well, there'd have to be more in it for me than lolly on a stick. But Elvis never tells you much, not before a job. He'd been all right when I'd done things for him before. So I said OK.

'Right,' says Elvis. 'Listen! We'll tell you how to get to

Hampstead Lane. There's a big old tree opposite a letter-box. Wait there. By the time we give you this wash-bag there'll be a bus at the bus stop.'

'Go on!' I said, 'How do you know about the bus?'

'That's the clever bit,' says Elvis. 'We've got a mate at the bus station and we'll have it all checked out. No one's ever done it this way before. Don't you worry, all you got to do is get on the bus, change to a forty-one at Hornsey Rise, and stick on that one to the end of the run. That's Tottenham Hale, and you'll see the laundrette just by the bus stop. Marilyn'll be there, long blonde hair, jeans. Give her the bag and Bob's your uncle. Only thing you have to remember is the forty-one bus.'

'Draw me it,' I told him.

Shane laughed at me. 'What did I say?' he says. 'You want someone who can tell a bus from the backside of an elephant. This kid's thick – *ouch!*' I'd got him on the shins under the table. Nobody calls me thick and gets away with it.

'He's not thick,' says Elvis. 'He's got *reading difficulties*. That's what his teachers say. When they can get hold of him.'

'I've not got difficulties!' I shouted at him. 'It's them letters and figures have got difficulties.'

Elvis was writing letters on the fag packet. They looked like this.

INBOG
BOING
NOBIG
NIGBO
BINGO

'All right, Bingo boy,' says Elvis. 'Which one's your name?' He pushes the writing under my nose.

I gave it a look, but they all looked about the same. 'My name ain't Bingo!' I said.

'He's illegiterate', says Shane.

'That's enough from you,' says Elvis to Shane, pretty sharp. 'He's in on this job.'

He drew some figures on the fag packet. A straight line. Then two lines meeting and a line across the bottom one.

'What's that then?' he asks me.

'That's a one and that's a four,' I told him. I'm not that daft!

'Right,' he says. 'Forty one.'

I put the fag packet in my pocket.

'We don't want nothing wrote on paper,' says Shane.

'Don't worry,' I told him. 'Any trouble, and I'll eat it.'

'Who says there'll be trouble?' Elvis asked. 'There's no law against taking a laundry bag to Tottenham Hale.'

2·IN THE BAG

So there I was, three days later, under this tree in Hampstead Lane. Trees, they're all right for the little dicky birds in the summer, with all the leaves on. But now the wind was blowing through them, and big drops of rain were falling out of them. There were more trees the other side of this wooden fence I was leaning against. I could see their trunks through a crack in the fence, but the street lights didn't shine very far in and it looked dark in there. I thought there might be wild things about. All right, who's scared of a squirrel? But there might be something bigger.

The posh people's cars went past, woom, woom, woom. They didn't care much if they splashed me with dirty water out of the puddles. A bus went past, and I knew there wouldn't be another one for a time. A panda car came along, not fast and not slow, with a couple of coppers chatting in it. I walked along in the rain for a bit as they went by. They don't look at you if you're moving.

But I thought, right, next job I do for Elvis, it'll be one of these fast black getaway cars.

I walked back to the tree and waited, and got colder.

All of a sudden there was a thumping and a crashing among the trees, and my heart went boomp-a-doomp. But I looked through the crack, and there was this white face and this black face coming out of the dark. It was Elvis and Shane, and they were breathing hard, and Shane was carrying a blue laundry bag.

I whistled through the crack and thumped on the boards and they came up to me on the other side of the fence. The way they were breathing, they must have had quite a run.

'All clear, kid?' I heard Elvis gasp.

I looked up and down the road. The lights of a car came round the corner. I gave the whistle that meant wait.

The car went past. I gave the all clear whistle. Shane's head came over the fence. He must have been standing on Elvis's back. He passed over the bag and I took it. Then he got on to the fence, pulled Elvis up after him, and they both dropped down into the road.

More car lights came round the corner. We started walking, not too fast, in the rain. I slung the bag over my shoulder.

I couldn't help asking, 'Have you got it?'

'Listen, kid!' says Elvis, getting his breath back. 'Those are your mum's best sheets in that bag. And my best dirty shirts. Don't lose them or you'll be in dead trouble.'

The lights were a bus, not a car. 'What did I tell you?' says Elvis. 'Timed it dead right. Run, kid! Don't forget, change to the forty-one, and the end of the run!'

I ran to the stop and got on the bus. The bag was lumpy, but it wasn't heavy at all. It felt like – well, a bag of washing. I could see Elvis and Shane walking along with their hands in their pockets, but I thought I'd better not wave to them.

The bus was nearly empty. I didn't like that, I felt everyone was looking at me. But the conductor, he was a black with a little beard, was counting his money and writing something on a paper. He didn't look up.

We'd only gone a little way when BEEP-BAWP, BEEP-BAWP, BEEP-BAWP, there was a police car racing towards us, playing the old tune on its horn. I could feel my guts turn over. A load of coppers shot past, the driver doing the corner like he was on a race track, and they went off BOOP-BURP, BOOP-BURP, BOOP-BURP up the road.

The conductor of the bus looks up, sees me sitting there with the dripping blue wash-bag, and says, 'Hey son, you didn't ought to go robbin' clothes lines this time of night!' Then he laughs so much at his own joke that he forgets to ask me for the fare. But I didn't think it was all that funny.

There wasn't a lot of traffic in Hampstead Lane, and I reckon the driver wanted to get back to the garage and nip off home to bed. He was taking corners almost like that squad car driver. We soon got away from the posh houses with gardens, and now there were streets and shops and lights, and I felt better when more people started getting on at the stops.

There was another bus ahead of us and I looked for the number. Most days, I'd just ask the conductor, but he'd already said that funny joke about robbing clothes lines, and I didn't want to make him remember me. I found the fag packet in my pocket and looked at what Elvis had drawn.

Elvis had drawn a thing like this on the fag packet 4. The bus in front had a thing like this, 4. All right, I know, I'd a teacher who'd swear blind they were the *same*. Well, they're not the same, are they? How can you believe teachers who say things like that?

I can tell you I was biting my nails, sitting on that bus seat. 'Only thing you have to remember is forty-one!'

Still, the fag packet and the bus in front both had a 1 on them as well as the other thing. You can't go wrong with that one.

The bus in front pulled over to the outside lane to turn off to another road. The bus I was on was going ahead. They both stopped at the traffic lights.

Right ahead, at the bus stop that my bus was making for, I saw two coppers standing. That did it. I nipped off the bus and on to the other one just as the lights turned green.

The conductor on the new bus called out, 'This is not a bus stop!' He was a black with straight hair. I took no notice and went and sat at the front where the hot air comes in. I put the bag on the seat beside me. The conductor came straight up for the fare.

'End of the run,' I said.

'Eighteen pee,' he says.

Eighteen pee! I only had two ten pees in my pocket.

I was going to say to him what about half price for age anyway. Then I thought: *there's a million pounds sitting on the seat beside me!*

I handed him my last two ten pees. 'Keep the change, my good man,' I said. But he rolled me out a long strip of paper and pushed two pee back at me.

I hadn't had time to warm up on the other bus but I was getting quite cosy now with the warm air blowing on my feet. And now I could think about what I'd got with me.

I thought of the picture, the way I'd seen it hanging on the wall in the old house. I looked at the bag and gave it a squeeze. There didn't seem to be room for all that knobbly gold frame in that wash bag. How much would a picture like that weigh? The bag didn't seem all that heavy.

Maybe it *was* just a load of old socks.

I squeezed it again. There was something hard in there. I can tell you I wanted to unwrap the bundle of sheets and have a good look. But the bus was beginning to fill up.

I looked out of the bus window into the dark. Outside there was this big castle, with all towers and that. If I had a million pounds – if it *was* a million pounds that I'd got – I could buy myself a castle. I wondered what sort of castle it was, out there in that bit of London.

'Anyone for Holloway jail?' calls the conductor. Well, perhaps I'd buy another castle somewhere. That place was for the bad birds.

We came to the road where there's the two big railway stations. Now I was rich I could get on any train I liked, go anywhere I liked. Go to the sea and get on a boat and sail away. Except I'd only got two pee in my pocket, until I could get rid of that picture.

If it *was* the picture.

We came to the bit where there's all buildings with big words in bright lights in front of them. I knew they were the theatres where you could go and see the rock stars and the actors and actresses. They were the ones with the money. But how many of *them* had a million-pound picture like me? I could buy a pop group, be their manager!

If it *was* a million-pound picture that I had.

The conductor called out, 'Piccadilly!' People got out to look at all the letters and pictures in bright lights. We went on and there were glass windows with big model jet planes in them. That was where you went to buy your air ticket to America or Australia. If I could get there, maybe I could sell this old picture, and no questions asked. But I only had this two pee.

The bus went past big glass windows with big shiny cars in them. I'd have a Jag and a Rolls to begin with. But I had to find this laundrette first.

Shops selling pictures! Maybe they'd buy mine. But they were all shut. And anyway, you don't just take the loot into any old shop, do you?

This bus ride seemed to go on for ever. Ordinary houses both sides of the road. The conductor calls out, 'Stamford Bridge!' That's the football ground, but nobody gets off this time of night. You know what? – I could buy a whole football team! Not *Chelsea* though.

Now there was a big bridge over water. Elvis had said something about water-works, the River Lea, near the end of the run. I stopped worrying.

I asked the conductor if we were near the end of the run. 'Next stop', he said. The bus was nearly empty.

We came to the stop and the conductor called out, 'All change!' I picked up the bag and got out of the warm bus into the cold street.

I looked around. Elvis had said all I had to do was get to the end of the run and I'd find a laundrette. And there it was, the laundrette, rows of white machines inside a steamy window. I'd done it.

I pushed open the glass door. It was warmer than the bus inside. A few women sitting around smoking, waiting for their wash to finish. Some kids fooling around, listening to a transistor.

Where was this Marilyn bird who was supposed to be waiting for me?

The black lady who seemed to be running the place came up to me. 'Can I help you, love?' she says.

'I got this wash, for Marilyn,' I said.

'Don't know no Marilyn, darling,' she says. 'Closing in half an hour. Last wash going in now.'

And she grabs the bag from me, opens the front of a big machine, and begins to stuff handfuls of old socks and shirts into it. And there's the big square thing all wrapped up in sheets going in too!

I had to give her a good hard shove out of the way and grab it all back again. You can't put a million-pound picture through the wash, can you? The colours might run or something.

'All right love, don't have to shove!' says the laundrette lady. 'Some folks don't want to be helped,' she says to the other women.

'I got no money,' I said. 'Not till this Marilyn comes. She's got blonde hair, jeans.'

'Plenty like that, dearie,' says the lady, moving off. 'Anyone know a Marilyn?' she asks the other women.

They shook their heads and their cigarettes waggled. 'There's a Marion something, comes here,' says one. 'Black hair though, always wears them long skirts.'

I was beginning to wonder if it was the right place. 'Is there another laundrette in Tottenham Hale?' I asked.

'Tottenham Hale?' they said back at me stupidly, and waggled their fags again. 'Don't know no Tottenham Hale neither,' says one of them.

There was an old man sitting quietly in a corner doing one of these crossword puzzles. They're like the pools, I think, only there's not much money in them. He says, 'Tottenham Hale? That's the other side of London. Right up in E four. Must be ten miles away.'

'Where's this then?' I asked.

'This is Putney, ducks,' says the black woman.

Putney! What was the use of Putney? That nit Elvis, with his number forty-ones and his fag packets!

'My brother said the forty-one bus goes to Tottenham Hale,' I said.

'I don't know about no forty-one bus,' says one of the women.

'But I just got *off* one, in the street there!' I said.

'Ah, that'd be a fourteen, wouldn't it?' says another. 'Not the same, is it?'

They looked at each other and one of them said, 'Don't teach them a thing at school nowadays, do they?'

Silly lot of old pigeons! I got that feeling like I wanted to kick in the glass fronts of all their silly washing machines.

'Well, how do I get back home then?' I shouted at them. 'I've got no money!'

'We've heard that story and all,' says a woman.

'It's what all the old drunks say, ain't it?' says another.

'Kids too, now. They're picking it up,' says another.

Well, I'd done it myself, for a lark. But now I *needed* it!

The old man in the corner says, 'There's a police station up the street, son. They'll see you home if you're really lost.'

And just then the kids with the transistor tuned in to the news and I heard the announcer say:

'... North London, and news just come in of a big art robbery. In a lightning smash and grab raid on the public gallery at Kenwood House, thieves got away with one of the nation's most valuable pictures. They abandoned the gold frame in the nearby woods, but there's no trace of the thieves or the picture. The value of the painting – one and a half million pounds!'

My legs went weak and I sat down on the bench by the drying machines. It was true then! Up to now it had been like a game, something between me and Elvis and Shane. But now it was on the news, and all the world knew about it. And it had gone up to a million and a half already!

I began to feel really funny sitting there in all the steam. I picked up the bag and went out into the street.

I took a few breaths of wet London air and felt better. But I still didn't feel happy. Ten miles from where I ought to be. Two pee in my pocket. Hungry. And Elvis would think I'd let him down on purpose. You don't do that to your mates when you're on a job. I know I'd been *thinking* of all the ways I could spend a million myself, but I hadn't really meant it. Not worth it, anyway. Elvis would be after my blood if he thought I was playing him up.

I walked up the street, not really knowing where I was going. There were all lit-up signs on the buildings, letters and words, they didn't help me at all. There was one, though: ⊖ . I knew what that meant: tube station. I walked up to it and I could smell the hot underground smell. You can go a long way underground for a few pee if you're clever.

On one side of the way into the station there was an old bloke selling evening newspapers. He had a poster with big black writing on it. For all I knew it was all about the big art robbery they were talking about on the radio. And on the other side of the way in there stood a copper.

Too late to turn round and run for it. I walked past that copper, feeling his eyes making holes in my wash-bag. But he never said a thing. I suppose they couldn't search all the wash-bags in London.

And I had another bit of luck. Inside the station there was a green ticket lying on the floor. I don't know how it got there, or where it was from or to. But it was better than nothing. I picked it up and walked past the lady at the top of the stairs. She was chatting to a mate and took no notice.

I got on the moving stairs and put my bag on the step. Down we went into the warm smell, past the pictures of birds in bras and panties. They didn't help me much either. I wasn't all that happy about going underground. All those stairs and passages and tubes with trains running to and fro. And nothing but words to tell you where to go. I didn't want to keep asking people questions, they might remember me.

I jumped off the stairs where the big comb comes slicing at

your feet. The passages went off right and left. I had to decide which. The old bloke in the laundrette had said Tottenham Hale was North. Which way went North?

There was a young fellow coming down the stairs reading a comic.

'Which way goes up North, mister?' I asked him. He nodded one way and went on reading his comic. I don't suppose he even looked at me.

I went on to the platform and waited. There was a sweet machine, but I knew my two pee wouldn't get me anything out of it. Probably wasn't working anyway. I wished I had all the five pees I put into machines and got nothing for.

I looked at the pictures on the walls. People down in the country with posh cars or boats or horses, smoking fags. Me, I smoke in the toilets at school, mostly.

The noise of the train came along, oom oom oom. The wind blew out of the tunnel. The little light on the front of the train came towards us out of the dark. The train came in, people got out and I got in. The doors slid together.

This is the bit I don't like in the underground. You sit there and nobody says anything, and through the window there's the dirty old tunnel with the pipes going up and down. And the stations come along and they're all the same, the same pictures on the walls of people smoking and boozing. It's not like up top where all the streets are different. You know where you are up there.

Not too many people got in and out. Most of them had their noses in their evening papers. Big art robbery, read all about it, I suppose. Then when they came to station they'd look up and read the name and get out if it was where they wanted to go. But I couldn't keep asking what station it was.

The train stopped and everybody got out except an old bloke who was asleep. The guard came down the platform calling out something I couldn't hear. He put his head into the open door and shouted, 'Edgware Road, all change!'

The old bloke on the seat didn't move. The guard went up to

him and said in his ear, 'Edgware Road, squire! We don't go no further.'

The old bloke opened one eye and said, 'Eshware Road? Don't want Eshware Road.' He was boozed. The guard shook him by the shoulder and said, 'Have to get out here, squire.' The old man got up and sort of fell out of the train. He wobbled towards one of those maps on the wall of the station and stood in front of it, rocking on his feet. He wasn't too boozed if he could read a map so I thought I'd ask him the way to Tottenham Hale.

'Topman ale?' he says. 'Who wants Topman ale? They can keep their Topman ale.'

I said, 'Tottenham Hale, mister. I want to go there.'

He turned to me and blinked. 'Poor lil feller. You lost? So am I. Tottenham you want?'

He ran his finger along the lines on the map, as well as he could. 'There you are,' he says. 'Tottenham Court Road. That's what you want, son.'

I didn't think it was the same as Tottenham Hale, and I told him so. He got quite narked. 'Kids, these days!' he says. 'Never satisfied! No gratitude!' And he wobbles off.

I sat down on a bench. I didn't rightly know what to do. If I couldn't get to Tottenham Hale I'd ask someone how to get to Camden Town. I could go home – though I didn't want to take the million-pound picture *there*, really. Well, at least it was warm and dry down here, but the station was very empty and there was no one to ask anything.

There was another platform through an archway, and someone was coming along it calling out something. He got closer and I could make out the words: 'Last train gone! Station closing! This station is closing!'

It must be the station master, and whatever I did I had to keep out of the way of *him*. Don't trust anyone in a peaked cap, it's a good rule – specially when you've got a million pounds to lose! He was coming my way through one archway, and I nipped out quick through another, on to the other empty platform.

Maybe he heard my wooden soles. They're not much use for

keeping quiet in. He called out, 'Everybody gone home?' and he stopped and listened. His voice went booming along the empty tube. I kept still behind a fag machine. His footsteps went away.

All of a sudden everything was very quiet. Something had stopped. It must have been the moving stair. There was a crash like a heavy door shutting at the top.

All the lights went out.

3·UNDERWORLD

I hadn't reckoned on *that*, getting locked up underground in the dark! I turned my head all round, and there was nothing but black, like my eyes had stopped working. I listened. Nothing except water dripping somewhere. I was down there under London, I don't know how far down. Maybe under the river, with the water dripping in. The tunnels do go under the river. And even if I called out there was no one to hear me. They'd all gone home except me.

I could feel the tiles of the wall behind me, the cigarette machine on one side. It was no use to me.

Then I remembered my lighter. It was in my pocket, one of those gas ones. Cost a packet – or it would have done if I'd bought it. I took it out and pressed the tit. The little flame shot up and it was so bright it made me blink my eyes. The light shone on the drink pictures and the fag pictures on the walls, but the tunnels at each end of the station still looked very empty and black.

I was alone, with my laundry bag. And the picture! At least I could look at that now.

I moved along to a seat, put the lighter down on it and began to take things out of the bag. I unwound yards and yards of sheet. It was a double one.

What I found in the middle was four bits of wood joined together in a square, with a bit of dirty old cloth nailed on to it. It didn't look anything like the million-pound picture with the gold frame and the glass front. Funny joke that Elvis had played on me!

I was just going to chuck the thing on to the railway line when the light shone on the other side. There was something coloured. I turned it right round and looked at it.

You know, I'd thought about that million-pound picture a lot, and about what I could buy with it. But I'd forgotten what it was *about*. Even hanging up on the wall in the old house I hadn't really looked at it. I knew it wasn't a horse or a cow. What had it been?

What I had down here in the tube station didn't look like a million pounds. There was just this woman and this kid. The woman's eyes seemed to be looking at the little kid and the kid's eyes seemed to be looking at me. There were some things flying around too, birds or something. Come to think of it, the million-pound picture had been something like that. It looked different without the frame of course. They'd been crazy to chuck that gold frame away.

I propped the picture up on the end of the seat, made myself a kip with the sheets and shirts, and lay down. Then I thought, the lighter won't last all night, so I put it out and lay in the dark. I was more tired than I thought I was, I must have gone to sleep pretty soon.

I had this dream about a wet furry animal walking over my face. I made myself wake up, but it was so dark I didn't know whether I was awake or not. I felt round and touched – a wet furry animal!

I screamed out, I think. I couldn't remember where I was. I felt the hard bench I was lying on, and it all came back to me, I was in the underground. The lighter, where was it? My fingers touched it, and I picked it up and pressed the tit.

The flame shot up and lit up the walls of the station and the dark empty tunnels each end. And little black shapes running away from the light among the rubbish on the platform.

The little black shapes turned round and looked at me with little red eyes shining in the dark.

Rats! And one had walked over my face!

I sat up, shivering, though it wasn't very cold. The light shone on the faces in the picture. It was like having company. I was glad I hadn't chucked the picture away.

Footsteps! Not rats' ones. Not boots. Pad, pad, pad along the platform, and a crunch now and then from a plastic cup on the floor. I looked up and down the platform. Out from one of the dark archways came a pair of bare feet, a shaggy body, a hairy face and head, and another pair of eyes, bigger ones, shining in the light.

I looked back and forth, wondering where to run. The faces in the picture were still there, smiling a bit.

The voice came from the archway, 'I thought I heard you scream. You OK?' The voice sounded better than the Thing looked, but I still couldn't speak or anything.

The Thing, person, whatever it was, moved towards me. Funny, I remember feeling I ought to be more scared than I was. I just had the feeling It was all right, even if it looked nasty.

'You're just a kid!' says the voice. 'Aren't you a bit young like to be down here alone?'

'I'm all right,' I managed to say. 'It's them rats.'

'Don't need to be scared of a few old rats,' says the voice. 'They're my buddies.'

Yes, well, some people have funny friends. 'Who are you?' I got out.

'Me? I'm Angel Jim.'

Angels, that's what the things with wings in the picture were. But they were all gold.

I said, 'You don't look like an angel.'

He opened up the front of his shaggy fur coat and underneath it was all glitter, in different colours. 'How about that?' he says.

'Where are your wings?' I asked.

'I don't bring them down here,' he says. 'They'd get dirty.'

I didn't know quite how to talk to an angel. 'Do you come here often?' I asked him.

'I got a pad down here when I need it,' he says. 'How about

you though. Ain't you got a home?' You know, he seemed worried about me!

'Course I've got a home,' I said. 'I was trying to get there but the lights went out.'

'Got it all together though, haven't you?' says the Angel, looking at the things on the bench. 'Sheets! And a picture!'

I'd forgotten about the million-pound picture, and I'd let this Angel see it! I didn't trust him, he had dirty feet.

'Just a bit of old junk,' I said. 'I was carrying it for a mate.'

Angel Jim came right up to the picture and looked at it. He smelt a bit. 'It's real pretty,' he says. 'I like it.'

He was going to pick it up but I grabbed it first, and wrapped the sheet round it. 'Well you're not having it,' I said. 'It's mine!'

Angel Jim sighed and sat down on the bench. He took out a packet of fag papers and some tobacco from inside his coat and rolled himself a fag. 'Would you spare me a light, please sir?' he asks politely.

Well, he never offered me a fag, but I picked up the lighter to hand it to him. I put it down quick. It was hot, after burning all this time.

He picked up a bit of paper from the floor and used it to light his fag. Then he said, 'Better put that lighter out. It won't last till morning.'

I didn't much like to, but I put it out and we sat in the dark. I could just see the red tip of his fag and a bit of his face. The smoke smelt good, but not like tobacco. I guessed it was, well, something else.

'What's your name then?' he asked. I told him. He went on smoking and talking, like to himself. I can't remember all the things, but he said, 'That's going to make young Ringo very unhappy. Saying "Mine. My picture. Mine. My candy. My bike. My motorcar. My house. My flowers, my trees, my sky, my moon, my sun." You see, young Ringo, everything's everybody's. Everybody's sun, everybody's moon, everybody's earth, everybody's food. Everybody's picture . . .'

There was a lot more like that. I could see I had a real nut there. Or I could hear it, rather, sitting in the dark. I held on tight to my picture. I guessed he was after it.

I even dozed off, curled up on the bench between him and the picture. I woke up again with a jump and he was still at it.

'Light!' he was saying. 'Star light, moonlight, sunlight, everybody's light.' But it was dead dark. Even his fag had gone out.

Then all of a sudden the electric lights came on full, and there were the shiny walls of the tube station, and the drink posters and the smoke posters and all the rubbish lying on the platform. It really hurt your eyes, coming on like that, after all that dark.

There was a loud crash from up top like the big door being opened, and voices and heavy footsteps came down from above.

'Come on then, young Ringo!' says Angel Jim. 'Don't want the station master to catch us.'

With all the lights on I could see that Angel Jim was just a scruffy hippie, of course. But better him than the station master. He seemed to know his way around. We nipped along to the end of the platform and found a little old junk room there, full of brooms and buckets. There was just room for an old blanket on the floor. Angel Jim must have been kipping down there. He shut the door behind us and turned a key in the lock and kept the key in it.

Footsteps came up to the door, slow and sleepy. The key jiggled in the lock. Somebody was trying to push another key in from outside.

The other side of the door a voice said, 'How anyone think I going to sweep the station when I can't get no broom? And the ol' lock broken.' The footsteps scuffed away outside among the rubbish on the platform.

We stayed in the little junk room, hours it seemed. The noise of the moving stairs started up again, and the first train came through. I sat on a bucket and fidgeted and wondered how long we'd have to stay there, but Angel Jim sat cross-legged on his blanket with his eyes shut and didn't seem to care. It sounded like a lot of people were in the station now, and another train came and went, and another. I gave Jim a push and said, 'When are we getting out of here?'

He opened his eyes and seemed surprised to find himself sitting in the junk room. He listened to the noises outside and then said, quite loud, 'Seems full enough out there.'

He got to his feet. I thought it would be better to wait till the station was emptier, but he grabs an old peaked cap from a hook and puts it on top of his shaggy hair, and pushes his arms into a greasy old rail-worker's jacket that was much too short for him. Then he unlocks the door, opens it with a clang, grabs a broom and marches out.

I followed him out with my wash bag, feeling that all London was waiting out there to jump on me. But there were just a lot of early morning workers standing about the platform, with fags in their mouths and their eyes half shut or stuck into morning papers. Jim swept a couple of squashed plastic cups off the platform with his broom, called out, 'Mind your backs please!' and nobody took a blind bit of notice of either of us.

A train was coming in. Jim threw the broom and the cap and the jacket into the cleaner's room, locked the door, put the key in his pocket and pushed me into the train. It was full of blokes in macs and overalls, and a few women. We had to stand by the doors. Nobody took any notice of us there either.

I asked him where we were going.

'How's about a bit of breakfast?' he asked. It didn't seem a bad idea.

There was a fat man squeezing me against the door, and he was reading a paper. I could see that Jim was reading it over his shoulder. Suddenly Jim lets out a great hoot of laughter, and slaps me on the back.

That laugh really did make people look at us. I mean, you don't *laugh* on a tube train, first thing in the morning. The fat man turns round and says, 'Do you mind? Something funny or something?'

'I see where it says Bishop Slams Streakers,' says Jim. I didn't see that it was all that funny. The fat man lowered the paper to give Jim a sour look, and then I saw what Jim had seen. And my guts turned over again.

I didn't need words. There on the front page of the paper was a photo of the picture. My picture. The million-pound picture, million-and-a-half, whatever it was. The mum with the kid, and the angels flying around. Just about everyone in the train must have been looking at it. And so were hundreds and thousands of other people on all the other morning trains. And the only one who knew where it was – was me!

And Angel Jim.

That only made two who knew where it was. But it was a lot different from last night when it was only me. He seemed to think it was a great big joke. But what was he going to do about it? Had I better give him the slip? Or had I better stick with him and see what he'd do?

He stood there grinning happily at me and the blue plastic bag. After a while the people in the train decided he was only some kind of nut, which of course he was. They stopped looking at us.

At the next station Angel Jim suddenly says to me, 'Come on, off!' and pushes me out of the sliding doors. We followed the crowds along the tunnels.

'Have you got a ticket?' Jim asks.

I said I had but I didn't know where it was to.

'Better than nothing,' he says.

This was a station where there was a big lift, not moving stairs. There was one little man who had to stand in the lift all day saying 'Mind the Doors!' and collecting the tickets. It didn't look like going up and down all day did his guts any good. But he actually gave a little smile to Angel Jim.

'Hallo Albert!' says Angel Jim. 'And how's the Great Big World Up Above today? The little old bluebirds flying in the sky, eh?'

'Drizzlin'' Albert sniffs.

'Albert!' Angel Jim coos. 'You mean the little dewdrops are giving all the thirsty daisy-roots a drink?'

'Tickets?', Albert asks, not very hopeful.

I gave Jim my ticket and he found another in his clothes somewhere, and he pressed them both into Albert's hand. Albert tried to look at them, but Jim was still holding his hand.

'These *good* tickets?' Albert asked.

'Al-bert!' says Jim. 'We give you what we can. Our best may not be very good. This little ticket is not, you know, an oil painting of the Virgin and Child by Pestalotsy. But it comes with our *love*, Albert.'

There was quite a lot more crazy talk like this, Jim standing there like he had nothing to do all day but chat up his pal Albert. But the other passengers started saying *they* hadn't got all day, and Albert drops his fistful of tickets into a box and calls out, 'Mind the doors!' And up we went.

At the top Angel Jim says, 'Have a happy day, Albert!' as the big doors open again. And, do you know, Albert actually smiles a little smile again? The lift opened almost straight on to the street, and there we were on the wet pavement, among people hurrying along with umbrellas and standing with long faces waiting for buses.

Angel Jim took a deep breath of wet air. 'Hello raindrops!' he calls out. Then he set off with the rain trickling down his hair and his bare feet splashing in the puddles. He turned up a side street and after a bit we came to a big building with brass plates and notices on it.

He went up to the entrance. I stopped. I didn't like the look of it.

'What's this then?' I asked. 'A police station?'

'Of course not,' he says. 'It's a fire station.'

'What d'you want that for?' I asked.

'I live here,' he says.

He looked more like a bloke who would *start* a fire than put one out. I said, 'I thought you lived in the tube station.'

35

He said, 'God bless the squire and his relations
        And keep us in our proper stations.'

I don't know what he meant. I said, 'What about that break-fast then?'

'Stick with me, kid,' he says, and walks into the fire station.

4·ANGELS!

I walked into the fire station behind Angel Jim. Inside there were big empty spaces, and the floor all covered with oil and rubbish.

'Where's the fire engines then?' I asked.

'They've built them a nice new home,' says Jim.

'What's wrong with this one?' I said.

He said, 'That's what we say.'

There was a big black round hole in the ceiling, with a shiny rod coming down out of it. I was going to ask what it was for, when something came sliding down the rod. A pair of bare feet, a white skirt, and a lot of hair. It landed on the floor and said a bad word.

'What's *that*?' I hollered.

'Another angel', says Angel Jim.

The other angel said, 'You want to get boots on before you come down there. It sure gives you a hot foot.'

I said, 'Can I slide down that thing?'

The angel said, 'You're welcome.'

The way up was a big iron staircase that rang as I stamped up it. All the windows were boarded up and there were only cracks of daylight coming in. There were rooms up there and there seemed to be a lot of people sleeping in them. At least there was a lot of long hair showing from heaps of old blankets and rugs on the floor. We went into a kitchen. There was a big old rusty gas stove, some odd plates and mugs, and a lot of paper bags. Jim started poking around in them.

'Breakfast!' he says. 'What would you like.'

I said I could do with three or four rashers and some fried bread. When he'd finished poking around he came up with two bowls of pappy stuff and some bread that wasn't even white.

'What's this muck?' I asked, polite as I could.

'Angel food,' he says, spooning it in. I was so hungry I ate some. Angel food! I'd like to see my mum give me that for breakfast. I'd give her angel food!

In the other room some of the other angels, or whatever they were, seemed to be waking up. Two of them came in through the kitchen door, stretching and rubbing their eyes. They were both wearing long dresses down to the ground, but one didn't have a beard so I supposed it was a girl. She had a ring in her nose. They didn't seem surprised to see me, just said 'Hi!' in a sleepy sort of way.

The girl angel picked up my blue plastic bag and started taking things out of it. 'Hey!' she says. 'Real sheets!'

I said pretty sharpish, 'You can drop that. It's mine!'

The girl clicked her tongue and gave me a soppy look. '*Please*, angel *child*!' she says. 'We don't like to hear you use that bad word. Do we, Marigold?'

Marigold seemed to be the name of the bloke she was with. He had these soppy clothes, but when I looked at him there didn't seem to be much wrong with his muscles. I didn't want to argue with him too much.

But I said, 'I never used a bad word! I said that's mine.'

'There he goes again,' says Marigold. 'Mine! Mine! That's twice already.'

They went on taking things out of the bag. There wasn't much I could do about it. The girl tried on my brother's dirty shirts and the fellow looked at the sheets and pillowcases.

They were coming to my picture. I jumped up and tried to snatch it from the girl angel. She laughed and chucked it to Marigold. I ran at him and he chucked it back to her. It was no use playing pig-in-the-middle like that. I stopped and said the worst word I could think of. But they didn't seem to mind.

Marigold looked at the picture. He just said, 'But that's *pretty!*' The girl went over and looked too. She said, 'That's really *nice!*' Not a word about it being worth a million-and-a-half! Perhaps they didn't know.

The girl propped it on the gas stove. There was a light burning there and it could have gone up in smoke. I snatched it off and said, 'Don't you know that's *valuable*? And it ain't yours!'

'But you're going to let us *look* at it, aren't you?' says the girl. 'That sweet little baby!'

I felt the frame where it had been near the gas flame. It had begun to get hot. 'You nearly burnt it,' I said. 'Suppose it had caught fire!'

'We'd have sent for the fire brigade,' says Marigold. And both of them went off into giggles.

Angel Jim says to me, 'Well, young Ringo, what do *you* want to do with it?'

That's what I had been asking myself. But these people weren't *serious*, like, about anything. I didn't see how they could help.

I said, 'Well, keep it out the way for a bit.' I couldn't go running around London with it by daylight.

'OK then,' says Angel Jim. 'Leave it with our stuff for a bit. Feel free! Come and go!'

I asked, 'What stuff?' and he says, 'Come and look!'

We went into another room where grey bits of daylight were coming in through cracks in the boards, and he turned on a light. It was like when the lights came on in the tube station, but what I saw this time was great big glittering wings hanging on the wall, and glittering stars and suns, and flowers and animals' faces and lots of long shiny dresses. Most of one big wall was a picture of trees and a blue river and a great red rising sun, all done in glitter. I looked at the little picture I was carrying and thought, *this* is the one that's worth more than a million? I don't know!

I said, 'What's all that stuff doing in a fire station?'

'We made it,' says Marigold.

'You going to sell it?' I asked.

'Sell it? No, darling,' says the girl and clicked her tongue. 'We need it for our show.'

I was beginning to understand. They were some sort of actors. I said, 'Cor, people would pay a packet to see a show with that stuff!'

They were clicking their tongues again. 'The show's free,' says Marigold. 'We just aim to make folks happy.'

Well, I couldn't make them out. They seemed a right lot of nits. But, well, maybe they were the only people in London who didn't want to make something out of my million-pound picture. I might do worse than leave it here for a bit.

So I hung it on a big hook on the wall. I suppose it was for the firemen to hang their things on. My million-pound picture just sort of disappeared among all the glitter. I began to think maybe the papers and everyone had got it wrong. Was it really worth all that?

Someone came padding up the iron stairs and into the room. It was the angel who'd slid down the rod. He was out of breath.

'Oh *dear!*' he panted. 'It's really terrible!'

'What is?' Angel Jim asked.

'Downstairs,' puffed the angel. 'All those policemen!'

The old guts went churning over again. Coppers! Just when I thought I could lay up for a bit.

'They're on to me!' I said. 'They're after the picture!'

'It's not yours then?' Marigold asked.

'He swooped it,' says Angel Jim. 'It's in all the papers. It's worth a million.'

'I never nicked it,' I said. 'But they can get us all for having it. Keep 'em out!'

'How do we do that?' Marigold asked.

A *gun battle up and down the iron stairs*, that was what I was thinking. 'Ain't you got guns?' I asked.

'Guns?' They seemed to think it was funny. They all went off in happy giggles.

I could hear voices and footsteps below. 'Well, *hide* it then!' I said. I was really hopping. These people never *did* anything.

Marigold picked up a big pot of gum and a bag of glitter. 'What are you going to do?' I asked.

'Disguise it,' says Marigold. 'It'll look great with glitter all over.'

The other angels seemed to think the same. Except one, lying in a corner with long blonde hair.

'Sure, that'll fix it,' she said. Or maybe it was a he. 'It won't be worth a million after *that*?'

'What d'you mean?' I asked.

'You want to ruin a priceless old work of art, go ahead. Who cares?' he says. Or she, or whatever it was.

'An knows what he's talking about,' says Angel Jim.

'Nobody's going to ruin my priceless old work of art then,' I said. And I went to snatch the picture from Marigold. But he pushed me off and said, 'Cool it, kid.'

There were some old posters lying about. He tried them against the picture for size. There were heavy boots coming up the iron stairs, making it ring, but he stayed really cool.

He chose a picture of an old grannie with a teapot. He slopped gum round the edges, folded them back over the frame of the picture and pressed them against the back so they stuck. Then he went to work sticking glitter on the teapot.

The footsteps were on the landing outside. 'Me and all!' I whispered. 'Somewhere to hide!'

At least there wasn't time to cover *me* with glitter. There was a big dragon's head in the corner, cardboard covered with paint and glitter. The girl with the ring in her nose said, 'In here!' and lifted it up. She put it down over me. If I scrunched myself down a bit it covered me all over and I could see out through the teeth.

I could see a police sergeant and three coppers standing in the doorway. There seemed to be a lot more hairy angels on the landing behind them. The coppers looked as if they wished they were a bigger squad.

The sergeant coughed. 'Morning!' he barked.

'Good morning, sergeant!' the angels sang, ever so sweet.

The sergeant came into the room, blinking at all the glitter as if he didn't believe his eyes. From where I was hiding it looked as if he was walking straight up to the grannie picture, where Marigold had hung it back on the wall. Bits of new glitter were dripping off it. *That's not going to fool him,* I thought.

The sergeant turned and faced the angels. 'Let's have no trouble, eh?' he says.

'Sure, sergeant.' some of the angels said politely.

'This junk,' says the sergeant, pointing straight at the teapot, 'is to be cleared out of here. Now! And you clear off with it. You've had your warnings from the Borough Council. No more squatters in the Old Fire Station, and that's the end of it. Get moving!'

Nothing about the picture at all! I felt weak all over now I knew they weren't after me. But I had to stay scrunched up in the dragon's head. If there wasn't to be a gun-battle, it would be a punch-up, maybe. There were a lot more angels than coppers.

But they just sat or stood around, going OOOOOW.

'Sergeant, it's *raining!*' says Marigold. 'You can't throw us out in the street.'

'That's just too bad,' says the sergeant. 'It's the street or the police station this time.'

'Oh but you're an *angel!*' says the girl with the ring in her nose. 'You mean we can choose? The police station will be *super*. This place is so *cold*. Come on, folks!'

And she started collecting up things off the floor and putting them in bundles. Soon all the angels were doing the same, singing happily. The coppers stood around, looking like they were wondering what they'd started. All this lot moving in on the police station!

The angels were taking down wings and crowns and animal faces from the walls, and putting them on. It was the easiest way to carry them, I suppose. But me, I felt a right Charlie, inside the dragon's head and tangled up with its red flannel tongue. I couldn't come out now with the coppers around. They'd start asking questions – even if it was only why wasn't I at school? Someone came to lift up the dragon's head, but I hissed, 'Leave me be!'

They finished doing up their bundles and lined up to move off.

There was the girl with the ring in her nose and a great big birds-nest on her head with shiny Easter-eggs in it. She was playing a tune on a penny whistle.

There was Angel Jim with a tall gold crown, a long dress made of strips of glitter, and two great glittering wings.

Marigold, with a huge spangled flower round his face, a lacy dancer's dress, and very tattered jeans coming out of the bottom.

Elephant faces.

Lion faces.

Tiger faces.

Giraffes.

All sorts of spongy fishes.

And there was the long paper dragon, with patched jeans and long dresses and boots sticking out from under it. I thought I'd better join that, so I scuttled across the floor and put myself at the head of it.

We moved off after the girl with the penny whistle. Down the iron steps we went, follow-my-leader. It was pretty difficult for me in the dragon's head. I had to hop from step to step. I saw one of the coppers watching me, and his eyes popped a bit, seeing the cardboard head come bouncing down the steps on its own.

They'd opened the big doors at the bottom, and we all marched out into the street with the penny whistle playing at the front. It was still raining hard, and soon there was water and red paint running down my neck. The policemen held up the traffic as we came out, and car-drivers gave us dirty looks from behind their windscreen wipers. Some tiny kids being pushed along in push-chairs pointed and stared at us, and I heard one of their mums say to another, 'Well, what's it all an advert for then?'

Then I had time to wonder where the picture had got to. It had to be in someone's bundle. I turned round and whispered to the front legs of the dragon, 'Where's the picture of the grannie with the teapot?'

Front-legs didn't seem to know, but I could hear the message being passed back.

'He wants a picture of his grannie in a teapot.'

'In a what?'

'A teapot.'

'His grannie wants a teapot.'

'Free what?'

'Pot.'

'Annie wants free pot –' It didn't seem to be getting anywhere.

I broke away from the front of the dragon and ran as well as I could up to where an elephant's head was walking through the rain with water running down its trunk.

'I want my grannie,' I said. I was doing it now! We were passing a bench by the roadside with a couple of old drunks on it. They stared at us and one of them threw his bottle of wine away into the bushes.

'The picture,' I said to Elephant. 'With the advert stuck on it. Where is it?'

Elephant was a bit more helpful. 'Maybe Orchid's got it,' he said.

I asked who Orchid was.

'That there octopus,' said Elephant.

I ran up to Octopus. 'Have you got the picture?' I asked. 'You know. The mum and the kid and the angels. Marigold stuck the grannie with the teapot on it. Some angel's got it.'

It sounded pretty mixed-up even when I tried to make it clearer. But somehow Octopus understood. He fumbled in his bundle and pulled out the picture. Then he passed it to me through the mouth of the dragon.

And I saw a copper was watching! But Octopus just said, 'Feeding time!' and laughed till all his feelers wobbled.

The line of animals and things came to a stop. There was a red traffic light, a part-time one where they were digging up the road. A big yellow machine was making a long trench.

I wasn't going to that police station if I could help it, and now I saw my way out. The trench wasn't as wide as the dragon's head. I went to the trench, rested the sides of the dragon's head on the edges of the trench, and slipped out of the bottom.

I ran along the bottom of the trench. A man saw me and swore at me. But then there was a lot of laughing and cheering behind me. I looked back. The digging-machine had picked up the dragon's head and was lifting it high above the street on its long yellow neck. It was my chance to get away without anyone seeing, anyway.

I nipped off quick round the corner. There was a sort of park place, and a shelter with seats in it. I went in and sat down. I needed to think a bit.

I mean, things weren't quite going like they were meant to. Angels and animals and coppers and fire stations – I hadn't reckoned on all *that* when I said I'd carry that laundry-bag to Tottenham Hale. I'd still managed to keep hold of the picture – but even that looked a bit different. And those angels, they didn't seem to care if it *was* worth a million. I mean, if you don't believe in *money*, what do you believe in?

Someone slipped into the shelter and sat down beside me. A voice said, 'Well, what are you going to do with it?'

I looked round. It was the angel called An. I hadn't given them all the slip after all.

'What's that to you?' I said. 'Do you want to sit and look at it?'

'I've looked,' he says. 'It's beautiful. But wouldn't you rather have the money?'

Maybe they weren't all daft about money.

'I thought angels didn't care about money,' I said.

He said, 'They don't as long as someone's paying them. Just now it's Uncle.'

'Who's Uncle?' I asked.

Instead of answering he pointed across the roof-tops to a big tall office block you could see for miles.

'How do you mean?' I had to ask.

'That's Uncle's,' he says. 'He pays us to keep out of it.'

'He must be rich,' I said.

'Very,' he says. 'And he likes pictures. He's a collector.'.

So that was it. 'He's not having this one,' I said.

'Why not?' says An. 'I guess he might buy it.'

'It's not mine to sell,' I said.

'But you've been saying it *is* yours,' he says.

'It's mine and my brother's,' I said. 'He nicked it: I've got it.'

'You'd be doing your brother a favour,' says An. Maybe he was right. Elvis couldn't say anything if I went back to him with a million. Well, maybe not the whole lot, I could keep what I wanted.

'I could call Uncle on the phone,' says An. 'Can you lend me two pee?'

It was all I *had* got. I said I'd go along with him to the phone box. We found one round the corner and we both went in, the picture and all. I wasn't taking chances.

He dialled, the pip-pip-pip started and he put our last two pee in. For a moment I thought the phone box wasn't working – like someone had been having a bit of sport with it – but then a voice said something.

'Hullo darling, it's An,' he cooes down the mouthpiece. 'I want to speak to Uncle Joe. It's personal.' I thought they'd hung up on him then, there was a lot of clicks and a long wait, but another voice came on and said something very short.

'Hi, Uncle, it's Anthony,' says An. 'I got something that will interest you. Like to send a car round to Cantelowes Gardens?' Then the old pip-pip-pip started again and that was that. He hung up.

'Is that all you wanted to say?' I asked. It seemed right dodgy to me. I mean, here was this scruffy hippie ringing up a millionaire and ordering a car.

'I've told him enough to get him worried,' says An. 'He'll send a car.'

We went back to the shelter. I wasn't too happy. 'Who's to say he won't ring the cops?'

'Not Uncle,' says An. 'Uncle doesn't want the cops around.'

He put out his hand to take the picture from me but I jumped back.

'None of your tricks!' I warned him. 'Or I'll take this picture and put my boot through it!'

I thought I had him there. It was like having a hostage. But he went off in that silly angel laugh, like I'd said something funny. 'Hey, let's *do* that!' he says. 'A million-pound kick! Wouldn't that be something?'

And he made to get at the picture like he *was* going to put his boot through it. I had to dodge round the shelter to get out of the way. And outside the rain was coming down in buckets. I was shut up with a nutter!

'Don't you know that's *wicked*?' I asked him. 'Smashing up a million pounds!'

He gave up and sat down. 'Smashing up a million pounds!' he says. 'That would be great! Still – that pretty picture, it would be a shame to spoil that.'

Well, I only hoped that Uncle had more sense.

Then I had to stop him from tearing off the grannie picture to look at the one underneath again. Fancy sitting in the park with a picture that was in all the papers! I wouldn't trust anyone round Cantelowes way.

But I couldn't stop him talking like he was selling things at an auction sale. He started calling out, 'Hey, people! What am I bid for Pestalotsy's Virgin and Child? One million? Two million? Did I hear you say five million madam? Going for five million!' But there was only a deaf old lady with a walking stick and a dog on a lead. They both gave him a sniffy look and passed on.

It was cold, but he'd got me really sweating. I had to get rid of him. Then he says, 'Here's the car.'

I looked round and there was the biggest and shiniest Rolls I'd ever seen. For some reason it was stopping by the gardens. He walked towards it and I told him to stop mucking around before we got in real trouble.

He just said, 'Come on, it's for us!' And the driver got out and opened the door for him.

'Good morning, master Anthony,' says the driver politely. He gave me a dirty look.

'This gentleman is accompanying me,' says An.

So I got in the back with him. The driver held out a hand with a leather glove on it to take the picture. But I wasn't letting go of it.

I sat back on the leather seat. Me in a Rolls! We were getting somewhere after all.

5·ANGRIES

The driver shut the door of the Rolls, and all of a sudden I knew: *this is what money's about!*

It was like he had shut out the rain and the park and the old lady with the dog, and all the traffic. Inside it was all quiet and warm and smelling of posh cigars. The driver got back in, the other side of a glass wall. Of course he was driving through the London traffic, but it was more like I was watching it all on a big telly screen. Buses and big trucks and little tinny cars, and people getting all wet on mopeds and bikes, and people waiting in the rain at bus stops. Silly nits, standing in the rain when they could be sitting back in a big leather armchair like me! You get used to being rich pretty quick.

I said to An, 'You can tell Uncle I'll have the Rolls anyway.'

He grinned and said, 'You'll need a bit of cash for petrol, and to pay Eugene.'

I asked who Eugene was. He said it was the driver's name.

'I reckon I'll get rid of him,' I said. 'He's driving like there's a coffin on the roof.'

I squinted through the glass wall at the speedo. There seemed to be a lot more room on the clock.

All the same we got to that office block quicker than I wanted. Glass doors with words on them. The driver didn't have to get out and open the car door, there was another peaked cap to do that. He held out a hand with a white glove on it for my picture, but I held on to it tighter than ever. I didn't go much on all these uniforms.

The glass doors swung open and we were inside Blue carpets and a sort of indoor garden. I think there were some goldfish. I felt a bit like one myself with all that glass round. Behind the counter a bird with shiny yellow hair looked at me like a cockroach or something had crawled in.

But they seem to be expecting us. The girl turns to Anthony and switches on a smile. I think she's the one that does the toothpaste on the telly.

'Executive lift, Henry,' she says to another uniform. And me and An and the picture got into a sort of space machine. Little green numbers blinked on and off. I suppose we were going up but it didn't feel like it.

This was a lot worse than the tube train. I couldn't even get out at a station if I wanted to. Why had I let myself in for this?

The door of the space machine opened and there was more blue carpet and a big glass wall with all London spread out the other side of it. Grey wet clouds, and office blocks with lights in, and traffic and people crawling along at the bottom.

There's a bloke in a posh suit waiting at the top, but it seems it's not Uncle yet. He shows us through a door, and there's a room that's nearly empty except a desk and some chairs, and quite a lot of pictures on the wall.

The bloke sitting behind the desk is reading a pink newspaper. I could see the front page. It only had one picture on it. But that picture was my picture.

The bloke puts down the newspaper and says, 'Well, Anthony, what is it this time? How much do the angels need?'

An says, 'This time I got something for you, Uncle.'

Uncle's eyebrows lifted above the top of his specs. An puts his hand on the picture I'm holding. But I'm not letting it go as easy as that.

'I'll give it the boot,' I said. 'I mean it.'

The eyes behind the specs looked at me. It wasn't a dirty look he gave me. He seemed to think it was funny.

'I may be able to talk business with your friend, Anthony. If he'll tell me what the business it. Perhaps you'd like some coffee?'

'I could do with a hamburger,' I said. I remembered it was a long time since I'd eaten.

'Three coffees and a hamburger,' says Uncle. There was no one to say it to so I suppose he was talking to a mike on his desk.

Then nobody said anything. It was up to me. Well, it was worth trying, after coming all that way. I thought of the Rolls waiting for me down there.

I went up to his desk and laid the picture on it.

He looked at the granny and the teapot and said something like, 'Mazawattee nineteen-twenties poster. I do believe it's genuine. Ruined of course.' He scraped at the glitter stuck on it.

'Not that one,' I told him. 'The one underneath.'

His eyebrows went up again. He picked up a knife from his desk. I think it had jewels in the handle but it was real sharp. He carefully cut round the grannie picture and lifted it off.

His face went sort of frozen. His eyebrows didn't even go up again. He gave the picture a long look. He turned it over and looked at the dirty old back of it. He looked at all the nails in the frame. He turned back to the front page of his newspaper and looked at that.

'I see the going price today is two million pounds,' he says.

My legs felt wobbly again and I had to go back to the chair and sit down. 'Two million!' I said.

He held out the paper to show me. Course I don't know what the words said.

'Doesn't mean a thing of course,' he says.

Oh. Didn't it?

'A thing's worth what you can get for it,' he says.

Well, that sounded like business. Like that lighter of mine. Good stuff but I couldn't sell it. Had somebody else's name on it.

'I'll be happy with a million,' I said.

He looked at me through his specs. 'I wonder if you would,' he says.

He seemed to be thinking hard for about five seconds, then he suddenly looks at his watch and says, 'Get me crackers.'

I didn't like to argue but I whispered to An, 'It was a hamburger I asked for.'

An whispers back, 'Caracas. Capital of Venezuela.'

Geography! I never got further than measuring the playground.

There was a knock on the door and a girl came in with coffee. No hamburger though. Uncle didn't try to cover up the picture on his desk. The girl's eyebrows went up and she went out.

We drank coffee. Uncle said, 'I'm not asking how this picture came into your possession. I can't keep it. I might just be able to find a buyer overseas. I suppose it's the real thing – if it's not he'll soon tell me.'

A voice came out of the desk, 'You're through to Caracas, sir.'

Uncle Joe spoke into the air. 'Hullo, Siegfried? How's your father? He's a wonderful old man.' There was a voice answering but it wasn't too clear from where I was sitting.

'Listen, Siegfried old man,' says Uncle. 'Would you be in the market for a piece of fine art? . . . About two million? . . . Usual terms of course . . . What's that? The line's not too good . . . You would have said yes yesterday? . . . Might think of it next week? . . . Yes, old boy, I quite understand. My regards to your father, and to Mrs Schicklgruber!'

Uncle Joe held the picture out to me. 'I'm sorry,' he says. 'My client says it's a bit too hot today. Keep in touch though.'

And I was outside the door with the picture under my arm, looking through the big window at the rain falling on dirty old London. My two-million-pound picture felt like a load of old junk again.

I hadn't even got that hamburger.

I went down in the lift with An. 'Why wouldn't he buy it?' I asked him. He just made a rude noise. I wondered what to do next.

We came out at the bottom. And there were all the blokes in uniform, and the girl with the hair, staring at my picture, all unwrapped. At least they weren't looking down their snooty noses now. They seemed to know money when they saw it. But I thought, *they've got to send for the cops now.*

I felt someone take the picture from under my arm. I was too choked off to do anything about it. It was the driver of the Rolls. His other glove waved me to the car. The doorman held the glass door open. I walked out and An and the driver followed.

The driver put the picture into the boot of the Rolls and shut it down with a clunk. He opened the car door and I got in, and so did An. The driver got in the front and we drove off.

'Where are we going?' I asked An.

A voice from nowhere sounded in the back of the car. 'Do not worry,' it said. 'We are going where the picture is wanted.'

It spoke so posh I thought maybe it was the voice of God or something. Then I saw through the glass wall that the driver's ears were wiggling under his cap and his jaws were moving. It seems that in these cars they put in a glass wall so you can't talk, then they put in a mike so you can.

'Where's that?' says An, beside me.

'I have friends in Somers Town,' says the driver.

An seemed to go even paler than he usually was. 'No!' he squeaked. 'Not *that* lot! They're really *rough*! What would they do with a picture?'

'They will think of something to do,' says the driver.

'How do they know we've got it?' An asked.

'They don't know,' says the driver. 'They expect jelly.'

Were we going to a kiddies' party? I didn't think so, even then. I'd heard of the other sort of jelly, that goes off *woomph!*

I could see An was really scared now. He starts banging on the glass wall. 'I'm not getting mixed up with this!' he squeals. 'Stop and let us out!'

'As you please', comes the driver's voice. The Rolls slowed down and came to a stop on a double yellow line.

An opened the door, got out and stood holding it. 'Aren't you coming?' he says to me.

And let the car go off with the picture? 'I'll stay,' I said.

An was going to argue, but a uniform came along the

pavement. It was only a traffic warden, but she seemed to make up An's mind. He ran off among the crowds on the pavement. I wasn't sorry to see him go.

The traffic warden came up to the Rolls, looked at herself in the shiny radiator, patted her hair and walked on.

I heard the driver laugh. 'They will never book a Rolls,' he said. 'Are you not getting out?'

'I go where the picture goes,' I said. I heard the driver say 'As you please,' again.

We drove past one of the big railway stations I'd seen from the bus yesterday. Well, I didn't know where I was going, but at least I was going in a Rolls already. We turned off along by the high brick walls of the goods yards. I knew I wasn't far from home. It would be great to drive up to the Council flats in the Rolls! With two million in my pocket!

Still, I hadn't sold the picture yet.

The car stopped outside a big dark building and the driver blew a blast on his horn like he was playing one of these electric organs. He got out and opened the door for me to get out.

'This is where the picture goes,' he says.

The whole street didn't look worth a million. Broken milk bottles and empty beer cans in the gutter. A lot of the windows boarded up. Right at the end there was a big blank wall.

A young bloke with a lot of black hair comes up from a basement. 'Ah, Mister Eugene!' he says. 'Have you brought jelly for the party?' He says that bit pretty quiet.

'I have brought you jelly,' says Eugene. 'And today some cream to put on it!' He's unlocking the boot, and he's wrapping up my picture in a classy sort of motor-rug.

Then the other bloke notices me. 'What's this?', he says, all suspicious.

'A little nut,' says Eugene. 'To go with the jelly and cream.'

I'd give him little nut! But he gets back into the car, laughing, and drives off. The bloke glares at me. He's standing there holding a box Eugene had given him, and the wrapped-up picture. 'Run away, baby!' he says.

54

Baby! I'd have hacked his shins for him, right there, only I was a bit worried about what was in that box.

'That's mine!' I said, grabbing at the rug.

You know what? *He* kicked out at *me!* I fell over backwards, mostly from surprise. But I wasn't taking that sort of thing from any grownup. I followed him down the steps to the basement and pushed in through the door before he could shut it.

We were inside a sort of kitchen. Two other people were standing up looking towards the commotion we made when we tumbled in. One of them, a young woman with long hair, quickly shut and bolted the door behind us. The other, a man in glasses, said sharply, 'Who is this person?'

He didn't seem too glad to see me, but at least I was a *person!*

'Eugene brought him,' said the first man. 'This too.' He put the box and the bundle on the kitchen table.

I made for the bundle. 'It's *mine!*' I said again. The man near me fetched me a wallop over the ear that knocked me into a corner. Nobody'd done that sort of thing to me since I got a teacher sacked for it! But I remembered what An had said: 'They're really rough.' Maybe they meant it.

I stood up in the corner and took a good look at them, and at the kitchen. On the table there were bits of a cheap tinny clock, pinchers, screwdrivers, bits of wire. The place was more like a workshop. But I didn't see where the money was coming from to buy my picture.

The woman was unwrapping the motor-rug. She made a sort of gasp when she saw what was in it. She held the picture up for Glasses to see, then to the other man.

The woman said, 'In the papers, they are saying it's worth a million pounds.'

I'd got my breath back. 'Two million,' I said. 'But I'd split the difference for cash.'

They took no notice of me. 'But how did it come into the possession of Eugene?' says Glasses.

'I nicked it, didn't I?' I said, pretty loud.

Glasses looks at me hard and nasty through his specs. 'You did not nick it, little boy,' he says.

'Well, my brother did, and it ain't yours,' I told him.

He keeps looking at me. 'Your brother, is he one of *us*?' he asks.

'Not likely,' I told him. 'He's one of us.'

Glasses looks at the woman. 'I wish that Eugene would keep to the Plan,' he says. 'What are we to do with this picture? And this boy?'

'We keep them as hostages?' says the woman.

Glasses looks at me like I was something brought in from the street on someone's boot. 'I think the boy is worth too little.'

'But the picture?' says the other man.

'Too much,' says Glasses. 'The police of every continent will be after it.' He sighed and thought for a bit. 'Later, we may use it. Now, we must hide it.'

'Until we have finished with the snakes,' said the woman. Glasses looked angry at her, like she'd said too much. But it didn't mean a thing to me then, what she said about snakes.

'You can give me a few thousand to go on with,' I said.

'Will you give this boy something to keep him quiet?' says Glasses to the woman. She opens a cupboard and chucks me a packet of crisps!

I was going to chuck it right back to her. but – well, it wasn't a million pounds, nor yet a thousand, but it was food. I ate the crisps. Onion flavoured, they were.

From the streets up above, but some way off, there came a beep-bawp beep-bawp beep-bawp. The three of them looked up, worried. Me too. But it died away again.

'Only an ambulance, perhaps,' says the woman. 'They are taking some old woman away to the hospital.' Then she seemed to get an idea. 'I know where we can hide the picture!'

'Where?' asks Glasses.

'There is an old lady,' says the woman. 'She lives in the street here. Number ninety-nine, top floor. Her rooms are full of all kinds of rubbish – photographs, newspapers, pictures. We will lend her one more picture. She will not believe it is worth a million pounds, and no one will look for it there.'

Glasses seemed to think for a bit. 'The boy will take it to the old lady,' he says. 'None of us must be seen with it.'

Well, that was OK! They were going to let me out into the street with the picture. After that they wouldn't see me for dust.

But Glasses seemed to see what I was thinking. 'You will play no tricks on us,' he says to me. 'Steven will be watching you from a window of this house. If you try to run away he will use *persuasion*. Steven, show the boy some persuasion.'

Steven, that's the bloke I met first, pulled back the dusty green carpet on the floor. It seems they kept persuasion, whatever that was, under the floorboards. He took up a couple of boards and lifted out a shiny black gun. I tried to look down the hole in the floor. There seemed to be quite a lot more there.

Steven showed me some bullets, and put them in the gun. And all the time that little round hole in the barrel was pointing at me. You know, that sort of thing's *dangerous*. It's all right having a bit of bang-bang on the telly, but people ought to be *careful!*

'With this gun,' says Glasses, 'Steven has smashed the kneecap of a young man. Is that not so, Steven?' Steven still wasn't saying much. He just nodded.

I felt pretty sick in my stomach. Smashing kneecaps, that's really rotten! I still didn't think they'd do anything to a kid like me, not really. But I wanted to get out of this place.

'You had better tell him what to do,' says Glasses to the woman.

'Turn right down the street,' she says to me. 'The street numbers are even on the right-hand side, odd on the left-hand. Go along to number ninety-nine, and you'll see the name Tomkins on one of the doorbells. She lives on the top floor. Tell her that Maggie has sent her a picture.'

'And come back and tell us you have done it,' says Glasses. 'We shall be watching you.'

Fine! Except that I never got very far with *left* and *right*, *odds* and *evens*. When people talk like that, I don't listen much.

'Do you understand?' Glasses asked. Well, it was the number I was worried about most. I was remembering what happened on the bus.

'Draw me it,' I said.

'Draw you what?' asked the woman. 'The street? The houses?'

'Just the number,' I said. 'I'm not too sure about ninety-nine.'

'He has a million-pound picture and he is not too sure about ninety-nine!' says Glasses.

'The kid is *thick!*' says Steven. I turned to kick out at him. I'd give him thick! But that gun was still pointing at me.

From overhead came that beep-bawp beep-bawp beep-bawp again, getting nearer. They all looked up again.

'We must get rid of this picture,' says Glasses. 'It brings us bad luck. Write him the number, there is no harm.'

The woman tore off the edge of a newspaper and scribbled 99 on it. She wrapped the picture up in the newspaper and handed it to me. I noticed she kept the rug.

'Have you any other questions?' asked Glasses.

'Will Mrs Tomkins give me two million pounds?' I asked.

He even smiled a tiny little bit. 'If she does, you may keep it,' he says. It didn't sound very hopeful.

Steven went up some stairs inside the house, and the woman let me out of the door. I was out in the cold street again, glad to be there. But I felt that somewhere in a window of the house the little round black hole of that gun was pointing at my back. I didn't know what I was going to do.

Actually, Steven couldn't have been watching all the street. There was a tree or two, and some big vans parked there. He couldn't see through them. But, like I'd seen, it was a dead end. I couldn't get out except by going back past the Glasses gang's house.

I walked along looking at the numbers on the doors. I seemed to get to the right one before I could make up my mind. I think it was my legs that decided to do what I was told. They didn't like the idea of smashed kneecaps. They walked me up the steps of this house.

I looked at the scrap of paper the woman had given me. 66, it seemed all right. What was the name they'd said? I looked at the little notices by the door bells. There was one, SMOTNIK, or something like that. It looked like what they'd said, near enough.

Before I could push the bell the door opened and a little girl came out. She looked at me a bit frightened.

I said, 'Mrs Tomkins?'

She looked puzzled, but then she pointed up the stairs of the house, and ran down into the street. Before she ran off she shouted something back to me that I didn't quite get. Sounded like, 'She's not switched on. Mum's sent me for a battery.'

I went up the stairs and came to a landing and a door. There was a funny smell, like – what was it like? Sometimes you go past a church and you smell this smell.

I knocked on the door. Nothing happened. I knocked again, and nothing happened again.

I tried the door handle. The door wasn't locked, and it opened.

There was this strong church smell. I called out, 'Anyone there?' Still nothing happened.

Well, you don't miss a chance like this, do you? Two open doors and nobody about. I went into the room.

The walls were covered with pictures. I could have helped myself to half a dozen.

Pictures, though – were they worth nicking? I'd enough trouble with the one I'd got. Still, maybe there was something else worth having.

6·DRAIN-PIPE

It was quiet up in that room, and the church smell was very strong. Funny thing, it was afternoon but the curtains were drawn together and there were all little lights in front of the pictures. Candles.

And a right creepy lot of pictures some of them were. A bloke tied up and all stuck with arrows. A girl getting cut up with a saw. Another bloke being cooked on a barbecue. One or two of that guy nailed on to a post. That's Jesus of course, but I don't know who the others were.

A voice said, 'God bless you, my dear!' It gave me such a jump I near hit the ceiling!

When I came down I looked round the room. In the corner, in a big old armchair, was a little old lady. All in black, she was.

'Put my dinner on the table here, please,' she says. 'It's one of my bad days. I can't move.' She talked a little bit foreign, but the words were all right.

'I hope it's not your spaghetti,' she goes on. 'Always they send me spaghetti. But your spaghetti, it's no good. Spaghetti don't travel.'

I didn't know what to do. I went up to her with the picture. 'Mrs Tomkins?' I asked.

She had a hearing-aid stuck into her ear-hole, but the works were hanging open and I could see there wasn't a battery in it. I remembered what the little girl downstairs had said, 'She's not switched on.'

I said very loud, 'ARE YOU MRS TOMKINS?'

She seemed to be looking at the words, not listening. 'That's right, dear, Mrs Smotnik,' she says.

Well, there's nothing wrong with *my* ears. The gang in the basement down the street had said Tomkins. This old girl had called herself Smotnik, clear as anything. I may get written letters mixed up, but not names when people say them. It was the wrong old lady.

I had an idea and went to the window. I peeped through the curtain and looked out. Down below was the tree that covered the entrance to the house I was in. And further up the street – yes, there was Steven. He must have come out to look for me. But he was way up the street outside another house. The one I should have gone to, maybe. I pulled the curtains together.

The old bird was looking at me and my picture, a bit puzzled. 'You're not the meals-on-the-wheels?' she said.

I knew what I was going to do now. I put the picture on her lap and said, 'It's a picture. For you.'

Her knobbly old hands undid the newspaper it was wrapped in. It took a bit of time. I said, 'You've won it in the old folks' raffle,' but I don't think she heard.

She looked at the picture. And she did something really comic. She put her finger on her forehead, then on her belly, then on her right side, then on her left side. I couldn't help laughing.

She said, 'The holy Mother of God.' Don't ask me what she meant by it.

The picture seemed to switch her into some foreign language. She went nattering on and it didn't mean anything to me. And she was crying. Well, the picture seemed to make her happy, anyway. Not exactly happy, but somehow it meant a lot to her.

She switched back to English. 'Thank you! Thank you! You are so kind! Such a beautiful picture!' She pointed to the fireplace. 'Put it on the mantelpiece, my dear. Where I can see it.'

There wasn't much room on the mantelpiece, but I took it and stuck it up there.

'Another candle, my dear,' she says. I found a dead one and I was going to light it, but she made me bring it to her. She lit it, and began some more muttering I didn't understand, then she made me put it in front of the picture. I thought of the angel girl nearly burning the picture on the gas stove, but I hoped it would be all right. These old girls get funny ideas. My old Nan had a room full of flowers in pots. Sometimes she used to let me water them. They never seemed to die.

I went back to the window and looked out into the street again. Steven was still slouching up and down the pavement with his hands in his pockets down there. What to do?

'You like a cup of tea, little boy?' says the old girl. Usually when people call me little boy I feel like lashing out. But, well, I reckon she was littler than me.

I said, 'Yes please.' Me saying please! But I could do with a drink, even tea. My throat had gone dry when they'd pointed that gun at me.

'Through there, is the kitchen,' she says. She pointed to a door. 'You know how to make tea good? Sorry, today, my legs are not good.'

I hadn't reckoned on me *making* tea for old ladies. Still, poor old bird, stuck up there in her armchair and nobody taking any notice!

I went through into the kitchen. Didn't seem to be enough food about to keep a mouse going.

I found a kettle and a tap, and lit the gas with my lighter.

Her voice came in from the other room. 'You find a bit of cake in the tin? Bring it in, we have some cake.'

Not a bad idea. But I was interested in the kitchen window. It was right up under the edge of the roof. I opened it and looked down. I'd expected some kind of back garden or back alley. But it was water.

A river? No, it must be the old canal.

Running straight down from the kitchen window to the water was a drain-pipe. I've been up and down some drain-pipes in my time, and I gave it a good look. It made me giddy. Three stories of bare brick wall, and the water at the bottom.

Was it worth trying, even to get away from the Glasses gang?

The kettle took a long time to boil. I didn't have to make up my mind right away. But the longer I looked at that pipe the less I liked it.

Of course I couldn't get down it with the picture. But I seemed to have given Steven the slip, by coming into the wrong house. And the picture would be as safe with Mrs Smotnik as anywhere else. I could come back for it when I wanted it.

The water boiled at last and I chucked a lot of tea into the pot and made a good strong brew. I even found a tray, and I put the teapot and cups and a packet of sugar and a bottle of milk on it, all posh, and carried it in to the old lady. I had to go back to find a knife and teaspoons. I never knew making a meal was such hard work. But there we were, having a cosy tea-party with the curtains drawn and the candles burning.

'You're a good boy,' says Mrs Smotnik. Me, a good boy!

'Talk to me,' she says. 'No one comes to talk to me.' It's not much use talking to somebody who's stone deaf, but I talked out loud to myself and it seemed to keep her happy.

'It's like this,' I said. 'It's along of them figures and letters and words. I mean, like the buses. Elvis says forty-one and I get on a fourteen. But a forty-one coming towards you, and a fourteen going away, they look the same! Leastways, I reckon they must. And on the underground. I had to get to Tottenham. But *Court Road* or *Hale* or *Hotspurs* – no one seemed to know the difference. I tell you what, half the people who *say* they can read, can't. And then they go and write ninety-nine on a bit of paper and by the time I get here it's changed. So what's the use of writing?'

'That's right, dear,' says the old lady. 'Have a bit of cake.'

I had some. It wasn't bad.

'Better than a bowl of pap and a cup of Nescaf and a packet of crisps,' I said. 'And that's all I *have* got out of me million-pound picture. Million and a half, two million, whatever it is. Even with the *money*, you don't know where you are, do you? Them angels, they didn't seem to care if it *was* worth a million. They don't believe in *anything*, that lot.'

I turned round to look at the picture. 'I dunno,' I said. 'Is it worth it?'

The old lady looked at it and smiled. 'The Holy Mother, she will take care of me,' she says.

'That's fine,' I said. 'She takes care of you, you take care of her.'

I heard footsteps on the stairs. I was out of my chair and into the kitchen quick as lightning. All right, I'd leave the picture in there among the others for a bit. I reckoned it was the last place the cops would look for it. But I didn't want anyone asking me questions – like what was I doing feeding tea to old ladies?

And down in the street I guessed Steven was still on the prowl. It was the drain-pipe for me.

I didn't give myself time to think about it. I was through the window and on to the pipe before I remembered I'd got my wooden platform soles on.

Ever tried climbing a pipe with wooden soles, even downwards? I kicked them off, but I shouldn't have looked down. They fell down three stories, hit a little ledge and bounced off splash into the water. Then they bobbed up and sailed away with the wind.

I felt pretty sick, that cake nearly came back on me. But I couldn't go back. I had big enough holes in my socks so I could hold on to the pipe with my toes. I let myself down carefully. Each time I came to a bit where it was fixed to the wall I looked to see if it was loose. None of it was all that firm. Shocking dangerous, the way they look after drain-pipes! People can get killed, climbing up and down them.

I did have time to think, *first time I've climbed out of a place and left it better off than I found it!* Two million pounds better off!

My feet touched the ledge at the bottom. It was somewhere to stand on. But where was I? Still pretty high over the water. The ledge ran along three or four houses to where there was a low wall. Further on there was a big black hole where the canal went into a tunnel.

I moved along the ledge. The bricks under my feet were crumbly, and there wasn't much to hold on to. The water down there looked cold and mucky, and I can't swim.

I'd got quite a way along that ledge when I saw a head poked over the low wall between the end of the houses and the hole of the tunnel.

The head was Steven's.

I kept still but he'd seen me. He was too far away to get at me, but I thought the next thing would be the gun poking over the wall.

The gun didn't come. Well, people don't go round shooting kids in London yet.

He looked at me. 'Well, aren't you the cool little devil? Where've you been?'

'I don't know,' I said. I was so muddled up about the number that I *didn't* know. I wouldn't have told him if I did. There were quite a lot of houses I could have been in.

'Come along and I'll give you a hand up,' he says.

'I'm staying here,' I said.

'And I'm staying here an'all,' he said.

I looked back along the ledge. It didn't go anywhere the other way. I didn't see how we were going to get out of this.

'Where's the picture?' he says.

'Try and find it,' I told him.

We looked at each other a bit longer.

After a bit he said, 'Who was it nicked the picture?'

I said, 'One of our lot.'

'Is your lot our lot?' he asked.

'Not likely,' I said.

'What about us getting together?' he says.

I didn't reckon Elvis would be all that pleased if I came back with a gunman. But what else could I do? My toes were getting cold.

It was just then that I heard a sound. I didn't know what it was, it was a sort of chug-chug-chug-swish. I looked back along the canal away from the tunnel. Round the bend came the front end of one of those long narrow boats that go along the canals.

It was coming at quite a lick past the ledge where I was standing. There was a good bit of water between me and it. If I'd had time to think I wouldn't have done it. But I did.

I jumped from the ledge, saw the water beneath me, and landed pretty hard on the roof of the boat.

There was an angry shout from the back of the narrow boat. When Steven saw what I'd done there was another angry shout from the side of the canal. He'd got himself on top of the wall and I thought he was going to jump too. But the boat had swung too far away from the side.

'Bring that boy back!' Steven shouted. 'He's wanted!'

I stood up on the roof to make a rude sign to him. Next moment something caught me a great wallop on the back of the head and knocked me over. I grabbed the edge of the roof to stop myself going into the water. Then things went black.

This is it, I thought. *I've passed out.*

Then I saw we were in the tunnel, in the dark. What had hit me was the archway, going in.

7·BIG VAN

I nearly jumped into the water again as the boat let out a great hoot. It echoed along the empty tunnel. There were lights in the front, like a car's, that lit up the mucky water in front and shone on the brick roof. The boat was going dead slow but the chug-chug-chug of the engine sounded loud in there.

A big voice boomed from the back of the boat, 'Hey, you there, whoever you are! Lie where you are and keep still! I'll speak to you the other end.'

I was glad to know there was another end. I couldn't see it. I lay there and rubbed the back of my head, and watched the bricks going past. It wasn't like the underground railway. No stations, no adverts. Just the chug of the engines and the slosh of the water along the sides.

I wondered if the railway went under the canal or the canal went under the railway. I wondered if it was roads or railways or offices or houses up above us.

I wondered why it smelt of onions.

Meat and onion stew. That's what it was. I was hungry again, even after the slice of cake. Perhaps it made me think of onion stew.

Away ahead there was a little half moon lying on its flat side. It seemed to grow bigger, and I saw it was the other end of the tunnel. When I got there I could jump off, like I jumped on. I didn't much want to speak to the bloke at the end of the boat.

Except there was that smell of stew. Of course it must be coming from inside the boat.

The tunnel got lighter and we were out in the daylight. Not very bright daylight, this day had nearly come to an end. A cold wind was blowing across the water. The canal quickly got wider and the banks were too far away to jump.

On one side there was a big square bit of water with tall old buildings round it. The buildings had smudgy old letters painted on them, and things like they used to hang people on sticking out of their sides. There were a few ducks on the cold water. I'd no idea where we were.

The boat swung round into the square of water and its front end got near the bank. It was time to jump.

'Hey, you up there!' came the voice from the back of the boat again. 'See that rope there in the bows?'

I'd seen a bit of rope. 'I'm not blind!' I shouted back. I looked back along the boat, and there was a big fat man with a red beard holding the thing you steer with.

'Jump ashore and tie it to the bollard!' he shouted.

I didn't even know him and he was giving me *orders*! Who did he think he was?

'Step lively!' he shouts. 'The wind's blowing us off.' As if I cared about his wind or his bollards!

I went right to the front and jumped to the bank. But, do you know? – I took the end of the rope with me. I don't know why I did it. Except, well, it needed doing.

I wound the rope round an iron stump at the side of the water. The front of the big heavy boat went drifting away, then the rope went tight and it stopped. It looked quite a thin bit of rope to hold all that boat.

The boat's engine chugged a bit more and the water at the back end was all churned up and white. The rope creaked and the back of the boat came in towards the side.

'Come here and catch the end of this!' the bloke called. *More orders!* But you might as well finish a job. I went back along the bank and he chucked a coil of rope at me. It hit me in the face and dropped back into the water. The bloke swore, pulled it back and chucked it to me again, all mucky and dripping wet.

That nearly finished me, but I caught it and tied it to another post.

'Thanks,' says the bloke. 'You've worked your passage and I'll ask no questions. You can push off now.'

I stood there on the bank.

'Well?' he says. 'What are you waiting for?'

'Me shoes,' I told him. 'They'll be along later.' It was cold and gritty on that bank with only socks on. I caught a whiff of the onion stew. 'Smells good,' I said.

The man shrugged his shoulders. 'Come aboard!' he says, and went down inside the boat.

I hopped back on again and followed him down. It was more like a little house down there, a kitchen with food cupboards and racks for plates and pots. There was a gas stove with a pot bubbling on it, and a thing to stop it sliding off if the boat wobbled. And this smell of stew, so good that it hurt.

The big bloke was washing his hands at a basin. He had to pump the water up into it with a thing he worked with his foot. I don't go much on washing my hands, but when he finished I had a go with the foot pump and washed off quite a lot of the green stuff from the canal. The rest came off on the towel.

The big fellow wasn't saying anything. He was putting plates and things on a table, and a long thin loaf of bread and some glasses and a bottle with a cork in it. He pulled out the cork, put the bottle back on the table and turned back to the stove.

I picked up the bottle and sniffed it. It was wine, like the old drunks drink in the park. I tipped up the bottle to have a swig. He turned round and snatched the bottle from me, then poured out two glasses.

'You won't like it', he says. 'But you can at least drink it out of a glass.'

He lifted his glass. 'They call me Big Van,' he says.

I lifted mine. I said, 'They call me Ringo.'

He drank and said, 'Ah!' as if he liked it.

I drank some. I went to spit it out on the floor. But I saw the look in his eye so I spat in the basin. It tasted like sucking a two pee bit.

Big Van ladled out two plates of stew from the pot on the stove and broke off two bits of bread from the long loaf. We ate. It was good. I polished off a plateful and sat looking at the pot on the stove. I knew there was plenty in it. He got up and ladled me out some more.

I didn't feel like talking until I'd finished the second plateful. Then I asked, 'Are you a bargee?'

'I am not a bargee,' he says. 'Neither is this a barge. This is a narrow boat.'

He went quiet again, eating away and drinking his wine. He got out some cheese and put it on his bread. He offered me some, but it smelt too much like the canal.

There was another smell, too. Now that I wasn't so hungry I noticed it. 'What's that funny smell?' I asked.

He sniffed. He got up and looked at the gas cooker and sniffed it. 'I don't smell anything funny,' he says.

It was a pretty strong pong. I remembered what it was. 'Turps,' I said.

'I beg your pardon?' he says. 'Oh, turps. Yes, you'd notice that.'

'Doing some painting?' I asked. Bits of the boat, outside and inside, were all coloured flowers and birds and things, I'd noticed.

'I do a bit of painting,' he says. He didn't say much, this bloke. He got up and made some coffee, and poured some for both of us. I put a lot of sugar in mine and it wasn't bad.

He sat back and burped. 'I'd show you some paintings if I thought you'd be the least bit interested,' he says.

'Who says I'm not interested in paintings?' I said. I didn't like the snooty way he'd said that.

'No doubt you do those hideous scrawls at school,' he said.

'Who, me?' I said. 'Art lessons? Not likely! I go and have a smoke in the toilet.'

Big Van was lighting up a dirty great pipe. But he smiled for the first time, between puffs of strong smoke.

70

'Quite right too,' he says. 'Art for the millions, it's a waste of time. What's your interest then?'

For a moment I thought he was on to me. I don't know what he meant about art for the millions. But I could tell him about millions for art. I remembered the word An had used about his uncle.

'I'm a collector,' I said.

He really thought that was funny, I don't know why. He laughed so loud the little jars on the shelves rattled.

'Excellent!' he says, slapping his fat knees. 'Then, if you've finished eating, we'll make a little tour of the studio.'

He squeezed out from behind the table, and with a glass in his hand and his pipe in his mouth he went to a door and opened it. A strong smell of paint and turps came out.

He put on a light, and there was a long long room with racks and stacks of pictures without frames on, and a big sort of stand with a picture half done on it, and tubes like toothpaste, and hundreds of little pots and jars and bottles and paint brushes.

'What's this then?' I asked. 'A picture factory?'

He didn't seem to like me saying that. But he pulled a face and said, 'You might call it that.'

'You never done all them pictures yourself, did you, mister?' I asked.

'A good question,' he says. 'I didn't do *all* of *all* of them.'

He pulls a few out of the rack and plonks them in front of me. I could see what they were meant to be like, but they were only bottles and fruits and dead fish. 'I don't go much on them,' I said.

'Nor did anyone else,' he says. 'I was young when I did them, but it's all my own work.'

'I know a pavement artist,' I said. 'He says it's all his own work. It ain't, but he gets a good few coppers.'

'I dare say,' says Big Van. He puts out some more. They didn't look like anything much, though I thought I saw a guitar in one of them.

'I wouldn't give you two pee for 'em,' I said.

'You'd be surprised,' he says. 'I painted them and put some-one else's name on them. Lived on them for years until someone rumbled me.'

He shows me another. I could see what it was about all right. Two old cows in a puddle, a bit like some of the pictures I'd seen in the old house.

'I became wiser,' says Big Van. 'I bought pictures in junk shops, cleaned them up a bit, and put different names on them. They brought me enough money to buy this boat. Easy work, but it made a lot of people happy.'

'My uncle Fred was an artist,' I said. I'd just remembered him. 'He made a lot of money. Couldn't spend it though. They *looked* home-made, his five-pound notes.'

Big Van was standing holding another picture, with his back to me.

'What you got there?' I asked.

But he went on talking, like to himself. 'Vandergraft's master-piece. I put all I knew into that picture. Paints, glazes, varnish. Canvas, frame and nails. Like the real thing, or better. And the brushwork! Pestalozzi himself would say it was his own.'

What was he on about? I caught a glimpse of what he was holding. 'Hey, let's have a look then!' I said.

I made a grab at it. I couldn't believe my eyes.

'That's my picture!' I hollered.

'I beg your pardon, young man?' says Big Van. But I'd got it out of his hands. Same Mum, same kid, same angels! I turned it over. Same mucky old back with writing on it. I'd lived with it long enough, it seemed all my life. But I'd left it up in Mrs Smotnik's room!

'There may be other copies of this picture,' says Big Van. 'But there's none as good as that. I spent a year in a museum doing it. Longer than Pestalozzi spent on the first one. In some ways it's a better job.'

'Then it's worth two million and all!' I said.

'An honest copy by Big John Vandergraft?' he says. 'I might get a hundred for it.'

I looked at it again. 'But what's the *diffcrence*?' I asked.

He sucked a lot more smoke out of his pipe. 'Er – one million, nine hundred and ninety-nine thousand, nine hundred pounds.'

And it was just then that we heard a thumping on the back end of the boat and a voice calling, 'Anyone below?'

'Visitors, this time of night?' said Big Van. His bushy red eyebrows came down over his eyes. 'No peace – not even in City Road Basin!'

I didn't like the sound of that knock either. It sounded too much like a copper's.

He went back to the steps and I put the copy of the painting on to the stand and followed him. At the top of the steps I could see a pair of black trousers and boots. It was a copper all right. His voice came down from above. 'Mr Vandergraft?' he asked.

'That's me,' says Big Van. 'Come down.'

I felt I ought to hide. But where could I, on that boat? Anyway, I'd got nothing on me.

The copper came down the steps. He was a young one with a beard. He looked at Big Van's bushy one, like he wished he could grow one like it.

'Sit down,' says Big Van.

'That's all right, sir, I'm happy standing,' says the copper. He straightens himself up and catches his helmet a wallop on the ceiling. He changes his mind and sits down.

He looks at me, a bit red in the face, and says, 'Your little boy?'

Watch it Ringo, I told myself, *you don't kick coppers.* Besides, I'd got no shoes on.

'My nephew Frederick,' says Big Van, without blinking. 'How can we help you, officer?'

'Sorry to trouble you, sir,' says the copper. 'Routine enquiries about the theft of a picture.'

'Have they lost another one?' Big Van asked. 'Delighted to hear it. Every Old Master lost means a chance for us struggling youngsters.'

'I understand you have some pictures on board, sir,' says the copper.

'Of course I've got pictures on board,' says Big Van. 'What d'you think I keep here? Ducks?'

'Do you mind if I have a look at them?' the copper asks. I thought, *now we're in for trouble!* But Big Van just says, 'Delighted! The gallery's open to the public.' He waved towards the other door.

'You'd better lead the way,' says the copper. He didn't want to turn his back on us. Big Van got up and went to the door. I went with him, and on the way he gives me a big wink.

The copper follows us through the door and ducks his head so as not to bang it on the ceiling again. Big Van pushes me to one side so the copper could get a better view, and so we could get a view of him.

That copper's face was better than all the pictures! You know, he was the sort who fancies himself battling with gangs of villains. And he's been sent down to a mucky old boat on the canal to look at pictures. And *there it is!* The million-pound picture. Staring him in the face.

He looks at the picture and he looks at Big Van. Big Van's puffing away on his pipe and not helping him at all.

He looks at me. I'm doing my best not to bust myself laughing.

He marches up to the stand, coughs quite a lot, and gets out the words, 'You don't mind if I examine this painting, sir?'

He puts on his gloves, white ones! He picks up the picture and turns it round. Then he pulls out a printed paper from his pocket and looks at it and looks at the picture, and you could see he was trying to make up his mind if it was the right one.

He turns round at last and faces Big Van. He says, 'Can you account for the presence of this picture on your premises – er, vessel – Mr Vandergraft?'

'Certainly,' says Big Van. 'I painted it.'

You could see he wasn't going to swallow *that* one.

'Are you aware, sir,' asks the copper, 'that this painting

answers exactly to the description of property stolen from the Greater London Council, estimated value one million – no, correction, two million pounds?'

'I'm a modest man, officer,' says Big Van. 'I don't value anything I paint at more than a million.'

The copper's face goes blank for a bit, like they do when they don't know quite what to do next.

'Would you be prepared to accompany me and the picture to the police station and answer a few questions?' he asks.

'What?' says Big Van. 'Walk along that towpath with two million pounds in the dark? There's a lot of rough people around.'

The copper looked at Big Van, up and down. He could see he was fat and not that young. Still, he was big. The copper looked at me. Maybe he didn't fancy being out with me in the dark either.

'Perhaps I could use your telephone, sir?' he says.

'This is not the Onassis yacht, constable,' says Big Van. 'We're not connected.'

'Then I shall make a radio report to the station,' says the copper. And he whips out his tranny.

He keeps his eyes on us, like warning us not to try any rough stuff, and calls up the station.

Nothing seems to happen. He makes the call again, and again. He gives the tranny a shake and starts getting red in the face.

'Have you got a screwdriver, sir?' he asks Big Van. Big Van searches around the racks of paint brushes and finds a screwdriver about two foot long.

He hands it to the copper and says, 'I expect this one's too big.' Big Van's face doesn't show what he's thinking.

'You wouldn't have anything a bit smaller?' says the copper. I saw a little one with a yellow plastic handle in a pot with some tubes of paint. I handed it to the copper. Then I wondered if I'd done the right thing. I looked at Big Van but he didn't seem to mind.

'Thanks, son, just the job,' says the copper. He takes off his helmet and shows a lot of red hair, quite long. He sits down at Big Van's work-bench and starts to take the back off the radio. I went close to him, to look at all the little wires and batteries.

'Maybe your batteries are dead, mister,' I said. He shook his head as he poked around. 'Tested regular, these are,' he says. 'We can't have them going wrong when we're surrounded by villains. Still, they *do* go wrong.'

'I've never trusted technology,' says Big Van. 'I'd prefer an old horse to pull the boat. But where can you buy a sack of oats?'

'What about that blue one?' I said to the copper. There was a little wire that didn't seem to be fixed anywhere. The copper looked at it and grunted. He shook the radio and a little brass screw bounced on to the bench and on to the floor. The copper said a bad word.

'I'll get it,' I said. I crawled under the picture racks after the little brass screw, but it seemed to have fallen through a crack in the floor into some water.

'Here, Big Van!' I called. 'The water's coming in!'

'It always does in these old boats,' says Big Van. 'It wouldn't take much to knock her bottom out.'

I crawled out. The copper was trying to fix the wire with a match-stick. He tried calling up the station again, but still nothing happened.

'They tell me you get bad reception down here on the water,' says Big Van. 'That's why I like it. Quiet. Like another world.'

The copper gave up fiddling. 'There's an animal feed firm in Corn Exchange Chambers, Seething Lane,' he says. 'I joined the Force to ride a horse.'

'You're a poet and all,' I said. He laughed.

'Have a cup of coffee?' says Big Van to the copper.

'I shouldn't really,' he says. 'But thanks very much.'

So back we go to the kitchen bit. Big Van heats up the coffee pot, and there's the copper sitting with his tunic buttons undone, talking about *horses*, and boats, and *art*. It's a real drag, and it's so warm and cosy down there that very soon I'm dozing off in a corner seat on the red cushions.

But before I'd quite gone off there was the tramp of feet overhead and a voice called out, 'Anyone below there?'

The young copper gasps, 'It's the police!', jumps to his feet, clonks his head against the ceiling again, remembers he's a policeman himself, and buttons up his tunic and looks round for his helmet.

'Constable Crippens!' comes the voice from up above again. 'Are you there?'

The copper goes to the steps and says, 'Yes sergeant! Here sergeant!' He turns to Big Van and says, 'It's the sergeant, and a couple of others. They'll want to come down, sir.'

Big Van shrugs and says, 'Let 'em all come.' And the steps are full of boots and legs, and the kitchen of the narrow boat gets suddenly very crowded with men in uniform and wet mackintoshes. And PC Crippens is explaining to his sergeant how he's cornered us dangerous villains and rescued the million-pound picture.

Well, you can't win, can you? There I was, at last, being marched off along the dark tow-path with four coppers, Big Van, and the picture.

Except, of course, that it wasn't *the* picture!

8·ARTY CRAFTY

That tow-path wasn't half gritty and damp with no shoes on. I said, 'You can't do this to me in my socks! I'll tell the welfare.'

The four coppers stopped and the sergeant shone his torch on my toes. 'This child's neglected!' he barks. 'Crippens, you'll have to carry him.' And the next thing I was piggy-back on the copper, holding on to his ears. Talk about police horses! I reckon he was glad when we got to a couple of squad cars waiting by the bridge.

They shoved us in. I was in front, between the young copper and the driver. I was looking forward to racing through the dark with all the sirens going.

Along we went, quite slow, stopping at all the red lights. I gave the driver a nudge and said, 'What about a bit of the old beep-bawp then?' I mean, it's no fun riding in a police car if you're going to stop at traffic-lights. But the driver just said I needn't worry, we'd get there soon enough.

The sergeant had the car radio in the back and there was quite a bit of talk to and from the station. That one seemed to be working OK. But I could only hear bits of what they said.

'Sir Derrick's at a dinner-party? I don't care, *send* for him . . .'

'You mean you haven't got rid of them yet? . . . Let them *have* the fire station so long as we can have the police station! *. . .* Well, keep them out of Sir Derrick's hair anyway!'

I couldn't make out what they were on about.

We pulled up by the police station and got out. Funny, the blue lamp over the door was shining on all bits of sparkly stuff on the pavement outside and up the steps, like little stars. It was all over the floor of the passage inside too. After a bit of talk they shoved us through a door, and I blinked. Among the coppers' mackintoshes and motor-bike helmets hanging on the walls were glittering suns and moons, and angels' wings. And all over the floor were bundles and blankets and tousled heads. The Angels were still squatting in the police station.

A blanket and some long blond hair shifted and Angel An sat up and blinked at me. 'Oh, man, have they swooped you?' he says. 'That's tough. I told you to keep clear of Somers Town.'

'You never told me nothing,' I said. 'You snuck off and left me to a lot of gangsters.'

'Did they get the picture?' he asked.

'No, I gave it to an old lady,' I said. I knew no one would believe it if I told the truth, so it didn't matter.

Big Van was blinking a bit at the glitter things among the coppers' helmets. Some of the helmets had got a fair amount of glitter on too. 'Very pretty,' Big Van was saying to himself. 'Very gay. Of course it's not *art*.'

An looked at him. 'You mean like it isn't little square pictures, man?' he says. I hoped we weren't going to spend the night at the cop shop nattering about *art*.

The door opened at the other end of the room and two men came in with the sergeant. I could see one was some sort of top copper in ordinary clothes, and the other was like an egg, dressed in that black-and-white gear that waiters wear.

The top copper looks at the glitter on the walls and the junk on the floor and says, 'What is all this, sergeant?'

'Angels, sir,' says the sergeant, po-faced. 'We've nowhere else to put them.'

The top copper starts saying sorry to the Egg, and the Egg says, 'I take it this is not what you sent for me to look at, Superintendent.' The three of them step over Angels asleep on the floor and go into another office. After a bit the sergeant comes out and says to me and Big Van, 'Would you like to step this way?' So we step, the same way.

The Egg was sitting in a leather armchair and the super was sitting behind a desk. Even from where I was put, I could smell that the Egg had been having a go at the wine that evening too.

The super was saying, 'I hope we haven't taken you away from your dinner-party on a false alarm, Sir Derrick.'

And the Egg says, 'My dear man, you did right to call me. I do so hope it is the Pestalozzi – ah, but here it is!'

The other door opens and two goons in white coats come in, carrying the picture on a sort of stretcher, like they have in ambulances. 'You see we're taking the greatest care of it, Sir Derrick,' says the super. 'Have you tested for finger-prints?' he asks the goons.

'I must insist that *all* tests be carried out by our *art* experts!' puffs Sir Derrick immediately. 'People don't understand how *fragile* these old paintings are.'

Good job I didn't let it go through the washer then, I thought. Then I remembered that it wasn't even the real one they'd got there. I looked at Big Van. He seemed to be hiding a smile in his beard as the two goons lifted up his copy in the white gloves and laid it on a white cloth on the desk.

Sir Derrick gets up and bends over it. The super, feeling he's been told off, says a bit stiff, 'If you would care to make formal identification of the property, Sir Derrick, we shall be happy to hand it over to you, and these two persons will be charged with unlawful possession.' Sir Derrick looks up at me and Big Van for the first time, mutters 'Brutes!' and goes on sniffing at the picture.

'Ah, yes, yes, yes,' he croons. 'There's no mistaking the real thing. I'm afraid there's no one living today who can use paint as Pestalozzi used it. And the *glazes*! Oh yes indeed, the hand of the master!' He turns the picture over. 'In case there should be any doubt, they just don't make canvas like this any more. Even the nails – they're hand-made. And of course we have Pestalozzi's dedication and signature. It takes a little practice to read this fine old Italian handwriting. But I'll translate it for you,

Superintendent. "Dedicated to the most magnanimous Prince Orsino by —"'

And the Egg suddenly goes off into a fit of coughing, has to be banged on the back by the super and given a drink of water by the sergeant. He sinks down into the chair at the desk.

'— by *John Vandergraft!*' he finishes, feebly.

There's quite a long silence, and Big Van still doesn't say a word. Then the sergeant looks across at Constable Crippens, who's standing in a corner trying to pretend he's not there.

'Constable Crippens,' says the sergeant. 'What did Mr Vandergraft say when you found this painting in his possession?'

Constable Crippens' going red in the face again, and he's looking through the pages of his note-book.

'His words were,' says Constable Crippens, ' "I painted it!" '

There was another bit of silence.

'It didn't *look* like a picture someone had painted,' PC Crippens goes on.

'That'll do, constable,' says the super. 'Mr Vandergraft, would you like to confirm your statement?'

'Certainly,' says Big Van. 'I painted it.'

'Then I charge this man with the forgery of a work of art, valued at two million pounds!' squeaks Sir Derrick.

'Was he asking that much for it?' the super asked the constable.

PC Crippens had his nose in his note-book again. 'The accused said, "I do not value anything I paint at more than one million pounds," ' he told the super.

Sir Derrick puffs. 'One million, two million, what's the difference?'

'A million,' I told him. That was an easy one.

'Aren't you going to arrest him?' Sir Derrick screams. 'We can't have live artists going round painting million-pound pictures!'

'I don't believe there's a law against it, Sir Derrick,' says the super. 'I'm afraid we've wasted your valuable time, sir. But I'm very grateful for your expert advice. We might have got egg on our faces – I mean we might have made fools of ourselves, eh?'

The Egg goes, 'Ooph!' and stamps out. I think he fell over an angel outside.

The super gives me and Big Van a long look. 'I still have a feeling you're up to something,' he says. 'But you'd better go home and keep out of trouble.'

'If you'll give us a lift back to the canal,' says Big Van calmly, 'we'll say no more about it, eh, Superintendent?'

Big Van picks up the picture and tucks it under his arm. As we walked out through the other room An sat up and blinked at the picture.

'Gee!' he says. 'Some guys get away with murder!'

They drove us back to the canal a good bit quicker than we'd come. Keen to get rid of us! On the way Big Van asked me if I didn't want to be taken home.

Not in a squad car I didn't! It wouldn't put Elvis in a good mood at all.

'Can't I stay with you – er, Uncle John?' I asked. I felt like, somehow we hadn't finished with his pictures. Maybe he felt the same.

When we got to the tow-path there was this shoe problem again.

'It's a shame to see a kiddie without shoes,' says the driver.

Big Van growls, 'We had to eat them, for supper.' And he swings me right up on his shoulders and walks off into the dark.

As we went along past the dark old factory buildings like that, I whispered into his left ear-hole, 'Here, Big Van, wouldn't you like to see the real one?'

'The real what?' he asked.

'The real picture, what old Pestypoxy painted,' I said.

He walked on a bit without saying anything. Then he says, 'If those were angels at the police station, I believe you're a young fiend of darkness.'

Then, as we scrunched along the tow-path, under bridges and along by tall brick walls, with nobody to listen except the wind on the mucky water and maybe an old rat or two, the talk went something like this if I remember it right.

'Where is it?'

'With the deaf old lady at the top of the drain-pipe.'

'How did it get there?'

'I left it there to get away from the gunmen.'

'And how did it get to them?'

'With me in An's uncle's Rolls.'

'And how did An's uncle get it?'

'He didn't want it. But I was in the fire station with the angels, hiding in the dragon's head and –'

The story was getting more and more difficult to tell. I wasn't sure why I was telling him at all. Anyhow he couldn't possibly believe it. I felt I'd had a long day.

'Suppose we sleep on it,' he said. We'd got to the boat again. We went aboard and he showed me a bunk, the other end of the boat from where he slept. I got into it and went out like a light.

I slept all right, though I did have these dreams about policemen flying about with golden wings and glittery helmets and egg on their faces, and being chased by a yellow road-digger with a dragon's head . . .

9·UP THE PIPE

Next morning in the kitchen of the boat I was scoffing fried bacon and eggs and bread. No pap for Big Van.

'Well?' I asked.

He was sitting quiet with a big mug of coffee and his first pipe of tobacco for the day.

'Well what?' he says.

'Have you slept on it?' I asked.

'Mmm,' he puffs. 'Your story's so preposterous I've decided to believe it. When can you prove it?'

'What about today?' I said.

'Name your time,' he says.

I supposed I'd have to wait till it was dark. Though how I could spend the time until then I didn't know. I'd be hopping to go all day.

He washed up the breakfast things – funny, seeing a bloke doing it! Then he gets out a tin of stuff and a rag and he starts rubbing up the brass handles and that, which were all over the boat. I watched him. It was sunny today, and the bits he'd done looked all gold in the sun. He never offered to let me have a go.

'Let's have a go, Big Van,' I said.

'Ah, well,' he says. 'It takes a lot of skill, this work. There are museums that would give a lot of money for some of these brass pieces. I like to look after them myself.'

'Don't be a mean old thing!' I said, and I snatched the rag and the tin from him and got to work. It was great, nothing to it. He

84

went off, smiling to himself. There was quite a lot of that old brass though.

When I'd done all I could see I looked around for him and found him where the pictures were, dabbing some paint on an empty picture. I sat on a stool and watched him at it. After a bit he looks at me hard, stops dabbing colour on the white cloth, and picks up a big bit of paper on a board and a bit of old burnt wood.

He goes on scratching at this bit of paper and looking at me every now and then. I couldn't see what he was doing now, so I asked him.

'You,' he says.

I hadn't asked to have my portrait done. I put on a scowl and scrunched myself up. He threw away the top bit of paper and started again underneath.

After a bit I couldn't stand him looking at me and I went over to see what he'd done. Well, I know I don't look *that* ugly! I mean, I'd had photos taken of me, I knew what I looked like.

I said, 'They don't cost much, you know, some of them cameras.'

Big Van says nothing. But he goes and unlocks a cupboard and takes out a thing that looks like you could shoot down jet-planes with it. He fiddles with a lot of controls, then he points it at me and shoots it off about a dozen times, from all angles. Then he puts it back in the cupboard and goes back to scratching away with his bit of burnt wood on the paper. Artists! I just don't understand them.

I got fed up with being looked at again, so I said, 'What about me doing you?'

He gave me a board and some paper and a stick of black stuff, but I said I wanted some red paint to do him. So he gave me a brush and a little pot of red stuff and I went to work. I tried to do his big red nose and his pipe and his fat belly, but after a bit I chucked it down.

'It never comes out like you want it,' I said.

85

He took a look at what I'd done, and he just says, 'That's true. it never does.'

I couldn't sit still, knowing what I had to do that evening. The drain-pipe! I tried not to think of it too much.

Big Van starts getting ready another meal. I think he was better at cooking than painting. I asked if I could open the tins for him but he didn't seem to have tins. Only mucky old spuds from the market, and vedges he had to wash the bugs off, and great lumps of raw meat. But it smelt all right by the time it was cooked, and it tasted all right too. I'd have eaten a lot more, only I was worried about that drain-pipe.

It got dark. Big Van started up the engine. I let go the ropes and jumped back on board. We backed out into the canal and started chugging back the way we'd come the day before.

The light in the front lit up the arch of the tunnel. Going into it this time I was snug in the back end with Big Van. But it still seemed a long time going through it, and my guts were doing funny things when I thought of what I had to do the other end.

Big Van switched off the light before we came out of the tunnel. Then he stopped the engines and we drifted out into the open. There wasn't much light out there but I could see the shape of the houses against the sky. The clouds were lit up, all yellow from those yellow street lamps.

There was the low wall, and the last house of the row. Where was the ledge and the drain-pipe?

We had to shine a little torch. There was the ledge. Had I walked all that way along it? I didn't want to have to do that again.

There was the drain-pipe. The boat was moving pretty slow, near to the wall where Big Van had steered it. He stood up to grab at the bottom of the drain-pipe, but he couldn't stop the boat moving.

'Give me your hand and hold on to something!' he hisses. One of his hands was holding the drain-pipe, the other one was grabbing on to mine, and I was holding a knob on the roof of the boat with *my* other hand. My arms felt like the big rope when the weight of the boat comes on to it and it stretches and creaks. But we managed to stop the boat moving.

We looked up at the pipe, disappearing up the dark side of the house. Way up above it was a gap in the clouds, and a star shining.

'Do you really want to go up there?' Big Van whispers.

I wished I could say I didn't. But it was my idea. I had to do it.

I couldn't reach the ledge. Standing on the side of the boat it was too high, and from the roof it was too far.

'Hold tight and make a back,' I whispered to Big Van. I climbed up his back and on to his shoulders, and I was on to the pipe.

I started climbing straight away. No use thinking about it any more. And doing it was better than thinking about it. It wasn't so bad.

I was at the top, level with Mrs Smotnik's window. Of course, I'd taken a good look at that window. I knew it would open easy enough. Unless she'd mended the catch since yesterday, and that wasn't likely.

I was on the outside window-ledge, holding on to the gutter. I slid the window down and climbed through into the kitchen sink. I knocked something over as I did it, held my breath and waited for the crash, but it was only a plastic squeezy bottle and it didn't make a noise.

I stood in the sink and listened. There was a funny sound that came and went all the time. It was the old girl snoring away to herself. She was making more noise than I was. Anyway, she must have switched off when she went to bed.

But there was a light coming from the living-room. Not a bright one, but I didn't like it.

I listened for quite a time. Cold water was dripping from the tap and soaking through my socks. But there weren't any other sounds. I climbed out of the sink and crept quietly towards the living-room door.

There was the smell of churches again. But still no sound, so I looked round the doorway.

They were looking right at me. Waiting!

The woman and the kid in the picture. The candle in front of them blew around in the draught from the kitchen window, made them seem to move. I nearly said hallo to them.

It was a shame to take them away from the old lady, I thought. But Big Van's would be just as good.

I went back to the kitchen, got into the sink, leaned out of the window and gave a low whistle. Then I took a coil of nylon cord out of my pocket and let one end down into the dark. Hope it's long enough, I thought.

I felt a bit of a tug on the cord, then three tugs, like a signal. I began to pull in the cord. This time there was a weight on it.

A black plastic dustbin bag came up on the end of the cord, and I knew Big Van's picture was on the end of it. I pulled it in through the window, undid the bag and took the picture out. I left the bag and the cord in the sink and took the picture into the living-room.

I moved aside the picture that was already there and stuck the other one up on the mantelpiece beside it, with the candle between the two of them. Two mums, two kids, smiling at me as the candle flame bobbed about. *No way to tell the difference between them.*

Then I went all hot and cold. Suppose I'd got them mixed up already! One was on the left and the other was on the right. But I was never much good at left and right, even with my own shoes.

Keep your cool, I told myself. One of them, the old one, the real one, had been on the mantelpiece when I came in. I'd moved it *that* way. There was a scrape of dust to prove it. *Must* be that one!

The stairs creaked!

I looked round the room in the candle-light, saw an old wardrobe in the corner, made for it. Then I turned back to the mantelpiece, grabbed the picture I hoped was the old one, and ran across and got into the wardrobe with it.

It would be daft to be copped now, I thought. Yet what was I doing wrong? I'd brought Mrs Smotnik two pictures.

There was a stuffy smell of old clothes in the wardrobe. But there was room enough for me and the picture. I shut the door on myself and listened in the dark. There was only a little keyhole, and I could just see the other picture in the candle-light, if I put my eye to it.

The stairs creaked again. There was someone coming right enough. But why were they so slow and quiet?

I hear a door-handle turn. Someone seemed to come into the room.

There was a gasp, and a whisper came: 'Holy Mother of God!' *Funny, it was just what Mrs Smotnik had said.*

There came another whisper: 'Be quiet, or you'll wake the old woman.'

And the first voice came a bit louder: 'Don't worry about her. She's as deaf as a judge.'

Two figures came into the bit of candle-light that I could see.

It was Steven and the woman. The Glasses gang! And only the thin wardrobe door between me and them.

'Is that the million-pound picture then?' says Steven.

'That's it, all right,' says the woman. Her black eyes wandered round the room, and my guts turned because I thought she was looking straight at me. 'And a good place to hide it, with all the other ones.'

'Cunning little devil!' says Steven. 'Hiding it here under our noses. Let's get it out of here!'

He picked it up and turned to go. But the woman held his arm and stopped him.

'No!' she says. 'We leave it here. Until we finish with the snakes. You just tear off a little strip.'

'What's the good of that?' says Steven.

'That is enough,' she says. 'We send the little strip to the Government. We tell them, send us the money, or we tear more little strips. They will know that it comes from the picture.'

'If you say so,' says Steven. He turned the picture over.

He was going to tear my picture! Well, no, not mine. I'd got mine with me, in the wardrobe. But he was going to tear Big Van's picture, after all the work he'd done copying it.

There was a ripping noise, and it *hurt*! I could hardly keep quiet, there in the dark. They just didn't *care*, this gang!

But I kept still as they went out of the room, and I listened to the creaking of the stairs as they went down. I heard the street door open and close at the bottom. Then I got out of the wardrobe. I'd had about enough of the smell of old clothes.

I went across and had a look at the picture on the mantelpiece. Steven had only torn a little bit off the back, as he'd said. I hoped it *was* only the copy. Somewhere among all that spidery writing on the back were some words that were different. But it had fooled the police, who can read and write I suppose. There wasn't much hope of me seeing the difference.

What about taking both the pictures back, to make sure? No, it would keep the Glasses gang happy if they knew the picture was up here. They would be searching for me, else. It would keep old Mrs Smotnik happy too. For her, anyhow, Big Van's copy was just as good. I was sure enough I'd got the right one.

I took it into the kitchen and put it into the plastic bag. I tied one end of the cord to it and leant out of the window and whistled. I could just see the shadow of the boat down there in the water. I began to let the black bag down into the darkness on the end of the cord.

Well, you know what happens to bits of string when you leave them alone for a minute. Funny how they get all cobbled up, no matter how tidy you leave them! I'd let about half the string out when I came to a great tangled lump. A right load of old cobblers!

I couldn't spend all night there uncobbling it. I did what I could and hoped it was still long enough. I went on letting it out. I came to my end of the cord, and the weight of the picture was still on it.

What to do? If I let it go it might fall into the water, and maybe get scrunched between the boat and the wall.

I jerked my end up and down to try and clear the tangle. I could hear the million-pound picture knocking against the brick wall down there. That wasn't doing it any good!

I should have pulled it all the way up and undone the cobble, but just then I heard *beep-bawp beep-bawp beep-bawp!*

Well it could have been a fire engine, or an ambulance picking up a bashed-up drunk somewhere. But that noise does things to my guts. I didn't think. I just felt I had to move quick.

I stopped to tie the cord to the back of my trouser-belt, got out on to the window-ledge, held on with one hand to the gutter and with the other to the neck of the drain-pipe where it bent outwards to the edge of the roof, swung off –

And the gutter gave way.

And there I was hanging from the neck of the drain-pipe over the dark water. And hanging from the back of my pants was

the million-pound,
million-and-a-half,
two-million-pound
priceless picture.
My brother Elvis's loot.
The National Art Treasure.
Old Pestalotsie's masterpiece.
Mrs Smotnik's Mother of God.
The mum and the kid – *don't let them go into the black water!*

I don't know where I got the strength from but I hung on. The bit of guttering fell past me, down, down, and crashed on to the side of the boat and off into the water.

Me next? No, I got my other hand and my feet to the pipe. All I could do for a bit was cling there.

Then I felt not quite so sick and began to inch slowly down that pipe. I don't know how I did it. Never mind, I don't need to know. I knew at the time I was finished with that lark. Never again!

Big Van's hands were helping me back into the boat. The engine started up and we slid back into the tunnel.

I sort of collapsed in a heap. But I remember saying, 'Open it up and tell me.'

'Tell you what, boy?' Big Van said.

'Tell me it's the real one.'

He undid the bag and pulled out the picture. He switched on the light and held the picture to it. He looked at the front, looked at the back, held it in his hands and closed his eyes.

'I could tell it with my eyes shut,' he says. 'It's the real one.'

I was very sick into that canal.

10·LOCKS

The first thing I saw when I opened my eyes next morning was little wriggles of light on the ceiling. I looked out of the window, and the sun was already shining on the water of the canal. I remembered yesterday, and I lay in that bunk with a snug feeling. Yesterday was all done with, and me and the picture and Big Van were all safe on board the *Rosie*.

Rosie was the name of the boat. Maybe *Rosie* and me and Big Van could steam away now with the picture, to South America or Switzerland or somewhere. Maybe they'd send cruisers and torpedo-boats and aircraft-carriers after us. I didn't know how fast *Rosie* could go. It didn't sound like the name of a boat that could go very fast. But I liked *Rosie*.

I got up and went to see if there was any breakfast. I was feeling pretty empty, but fine except for that. Big Van was frying bacon again.

'Ah, there you are!' he grunted. 'Put that inside you. We'd better be on our way.'

'Where to, Big Van?' I asked, with a mouthful of fried bread. 'America? Australia?'

'We might make Birmingham,' he says.

Birmingham didn't sound much of a place. 'Do we have to go in the sea?' I asked.

'The sea!' he says. 'Not likely. *Rosie* wouldn't last long in the wash of a Thames tug.'

Oh well, I thought, I don't have much luck with getaways. But, anyway, we'd be on the move.

93

First thing, after we cast off, we had to go out of the sunshine, into that old tunnel again. I was getting fair sick of it. Didn't fancy meeting yesterday's dinner. When we came out the other end I stayed down in the kitchen. I didn't want to be seen, and I didn't want to look, either.

But after a bit I went up into the sunshine. *Rosie* was chugging happily along through the green water, and the sun was shining on the old brick walls and on clumps of weeds with yellow flowers on the tow-path.

There was a couple of little ducks swimming in the water ahead. I went and got some crusts from the kitchen, and chucked bits to the ducks. Once they saw where their breakfast was coming from, they paddled alongside of us. They didn't seem to be paddling very hard.

We passed under a bridge. Buses and cars whizzed overhead, but nobody up there seemed to take any notice of us. Like Big Van had said the other night, it was quiet down here. Another world.

We came round a bend. I looked ahead, and straight away I called back to Big Van. 'Here, Big Van! We've run out of water!'

It looked like the canal had come to an end. At least there were two huge doors across it.

Big Van spoiled the quietness by letting out a loud hoot on his horn. There was a little house on the bank with a garden alongside of it. An old lady with her hair in curlers stuck her head out of the door and called out, 'He's gone to the doctor's. You'll have to do it yourself.'

Big Van steered the boat to the side and I helped him to tie it up to a couple of big iron rings.

'Do you know anything about locks?' Big Van asked me.

I said there were some you could open with a bit of bent wire, and some you could push back with a bit of plastic.

'Canal locks, I meant,' he says. I looked at the big doors across the water. Well, you wouldn't know where to begin on them.

We got out and walked up a slope. It was quite steep, and the canal started again level with the top. The little ducks took off from the bottom bit of water and flew up and landed on the higher bit. All right for them, but I didn't see how we were going to get Rosie up there. And there were these two lots of double doors across the canal.

Big Van took something from the woman, I supposed it was the key. Only it was more like a big iron handle with a square ring on the end. He fitted it over the end of a square bar on the door-post and began turning it. I once saw a bloke start an old-fashioned car like that.

There was a noise of rushing water. 'Watch it!' I called, 'You're letting all the water out!' Underneath where he was standing it was pouring out, all white and frothy. Big Van just laughed and walked across the top of the big doors and started winding the handle the other side. More water rushed out from that side. It made such a commotion that Rosie started swinging about on her ropes. I hoped I'd tied mine tight enough.

Between the two lots of double doors the water went down and down, and I could see more and more of the brick walls, covered in green muck. At last it stopped pouring out into the bottom bit of canal, and there was a deep slimy pit, quite a bit bigger than Rosie, with doors at each end and water in the bottom.

'Open her up, then!' Big Van called across to me. He was leaning on a sort of huge thick long beam sticking out from one of the big doors, and the door was coming slowly open.

All right for him, too! He was big enough and ugly enough. But me, shift one of those big doors?

I leant against the other big beam and pushed hard as I could with my feet in their socks on the gritty concrete. Like I expected, nothing happened. I stopped pushing so hard, but I went on leaning, and I felt the huge beam beginning to move!

'She's coming!' I called across to Big Van.

'That's it,' he called back. 'She'll come when she's ready!'

The two big doors were open. Big Van was winding away with the handle again. I could see now how it worked a little door at the bottom. When it was shut he came across and wound down the other side. Then he told me to wait there, and he went back to the boat.

He let go the ropes and started up and chugged slowly in through the doors we'd just opened. He called up from the bottom of the slimy pit, 'Can you get them shut again?'

I leaned against the beam and – when she was ready – the big door swung to again. I climbed across the top of the other doors, leaned against the beam the other side, and closed that too.

So there was *Rosie*, way down below me in the slimy pit between the closed doors. Fine! But, you know, I still didn't see how she was going to get up to the level of the water at the top. Or were we going to let all the water out of the top bit of canal?

'Do you think you can wind up the other paddles?' Big Van called. Paddles? Must be the name of the little doors that let the water through, It looked easy enough.

I fitted the handle on to the thing that worked the paddles on the doors in front of Rosie, and swung on it. It was a lot harder than opening the big doors. I was soon sweating.

'If it's too much for you I'll climb up,' says Big Van. But I shook my head. I was winning.

I wound one paddle open, and went across and wound the other one open. The water rushed, foaming white, into the space between the doors. And of course, as it filled up, *Rosie* floated slowly up to the top level.

Then all I had to do was open one big door, cross over at the back and open the other big door, wind down the paddle on one side, wind down the paddle on the other side, and jump back on board. And we were off again.

I lay flat on my back on the roof of the boat. I reckoned I'd earned my trip to Birmingham.

We chugged round another bend. I looked ahead, and sat up.

'Blimey, Big Van!' I called out. 'There's *another* one of them locks!'

Big Van just nodded, and his pipe went up and down. Do you know – we had to do the lot all over again! Opening the paddles, opening the doors, putting the boat through, shutting the doors, opening the other paddles, filling the lock, opening the doors, closing the paddles, driving the boat out on to the next higher bit of canal.

At least I was getting the hang of it. When Big Van started telling me what to do, I told him, 'I know, I know.' But by the time I was back on board, I don't know which had bigger holes in them, the soles of my socks or the palms of my hands.

I lay back on the roof again and called back to Big Van, 'Are there any more of 'em between here and Birmingham?'

'About two hundred,' says Big Van.

Two hundred! There must be an easier way of travelling! I lay back on the roof and watched a couple of long white lines streaking across the blue sky. Jet plane off to America, Australia, somewhere . . . I wasn't exactly in the jet set, was I?

But, you know, I just thought, *what's the hurry?*

I went down to Big Van's paint-shop and brought up a bit of chalk. On the side of the boat I started keeping a score of locks we went through.

I chalked up two more.

I said to Big Van, 'How about you opening the locks and me driving the boat through?'

'Getting tired?' he asked.

'Me, tired?' I said. 'I don't get tired. But it's a bit of a drag, like.'

'Would you like to go ashore and get me a box of matches?' he says.

It would make a change, so I said yes. Then he chucks me a fiver and says, 'Get yourself a pair of shoes too. I'll go ahead to Camden Lock.'

Big Van steered towards the bank and I jumped across and nipped up some steps. Funny being on street level again. But I'd forgotten to ask where we were. There was a street name up on a wall and I tried to read it. Scotch, was it – MacSomething? I looked to the right and stepped into the street, still trying hopefully to make out the name and WHOOM PARP SCREECH! I was nearly under a dirty great truck.

I jumped back in time, but tripped over the kerb and came down. Not so funny when you forget how fast the traffic goes. I lay there for a bit, taking a nice breath of exhaust smoke and saying some rude words towards the back of the truck.

A man and a woman bent over me. Greeks, they were, I think. 'Poor little boy!' says the woman. 'Are you all right?'

'Where am I?' I asked.

'He is feeling faint,' says the man. 'Better we get a doctor.'

I got up. 'I'm OK,' I said. 'I don't want a doctor, I want a shoe-shop. Where am I?'

The man said, 'This is Camden Street. Turn right, that's Camden Road, second left, that's Camden High Street. Plenty shoe-shops there.'

Left right left! Street road street! I never remember things like that. I ran off towards where the traffic looked thickest. I came to a place where about six roads come together, and there are red lights and green lights and yellow lights and notices that flash on and off and words and signs written on the roads.

I could see a shoe-shop the other side of all this – it had shoes outside it. I was still alive when I got across to it. On the rack in the street there were some shoes with big brass studs all round. I reckoned they could do a bit of damage so I picked out a couple about my size.

There didn't seem to be anything to stop me walking off with them. Some shops, they just ask for it. There ought to be a law against making it so easy. But as I was standing there wondering which way to go next the girl came out of the shop and says, pretty nasty, 'Can I *help* you?'

I said I thought it was help-yourself.

'Them two won't be much good to you,' she says. 'Not unless you've got two left feet. The right ones are inside.'

A mean trick! And anyway, why do we have to have left and right feet?

I flashed my fiver at her, and she says, 'Right, I'll see if we've got any left.'

I went in and tried on the other shoe. The girl wrinkled up her nose at my feet, and I don't think she was too keen on me trying on any more. But they didn't pinch too much, so I paid her. She put them in a bag and I took them out and put them on my feet.

She brought me the change. It wasn't much. I asked her if she sold matches.

'Matches?' she says. 'No, we don't stock them. Shoelaces?'

I asked her where you could *get* matches.

'*Matches?*' she says again. She turned to the other girl there. 'Where d'you get matches, Trace?'

'Noshco's,' says the other girl.

I asked where that was.

'Turn right outside the shop. Five or six shops down on the left. Can't miss it.'

Couldn't I? I'd have a go anyhow.

I don't know if it was Noshco's but I found one of these big supermarkets. I wandered in and there was a bloke glaring at me. Security guard, sure enough, the bloke who makes sure you don't stuff spaghetti down your trouserlegs.

'Wouldn't you like to take a trolley, young man?' he says, smiling with his mouth and glaring with his eyes. So I took a trolley, and scooted it up and down the counters looking for a box of matches. Big Van hadn't said anything about buying food, and I only had a few pee change.

I found matches, but they were done up in big packets. I knew what they were from the picture on the outside. I undid a packet and took out a little box and put it in the trolley. Then I went to join the queue at the check-out desk.

I felt a bit of a Charlie with my one box of matches behind all those mums with packets of Yummy Whip and Instant Custard, but I didn't mind much. I felt like telling them, *one day, when I've flogged that picture, I'll come in the Rolls and buy one of everything.*

They weren't all mums in the queue. Right in front of me was a young bloke with long dark hair, and a girl with longer dark hair. The hair reminded me of – I suddenly went cold in the stuffy supermarket. It *was* Steven and the woman!

I nipped pretty quick behind a stack of Doggo and Moggo. I was still near enough to hear what they were saying.

'I'll have to go on,' Steven was saying. 'I said I'd meet Eugene at the Rooty.'

'And leave me to carry the food?' says the woman. 'Aren't you the shovingest pig?' At least that's what I thought she said, it sounded rude anyway.

'I'll see you there,' says Steven. And he left the queue and made for the way out.

She called out to him, 'Where is it, this Rooty?' And Steven called back, 'Camden Lock!'

Camden Lock! That was where I was to meet Big Van and the *Rosie*. Steven had seen the *Rosie* when I jumped off the ledge. I had to keep *Rosie* and Big Van apart from the Glasses gang somehow. I had to follow Steven, get ahead of him if I could. And I had to get out without the woman seeing me.

There was a pile of empty cardboard boxes by one of the check-outs. I grabbed one and shoved it over my head, and made for the way out. I heard the security bloke shout, 'Hey, stop that boy!' But I didn't stop. I wasn't doing anything wrong anyway, they let you take these boxes.

Out in the street I chucked the box away. I had to keep Steven in sight and I couldn't see too well with it on my head. There he was, going up Camden High Street. I kept a few people between him and me, and followed.

I wished I'd kept the box on my head, because Steven suddenly stopped and turned right round to look behind him. I don't know why. Maybe he was looking back for the woman, maybe he was always worried about being followed.

I was outside a big posh furniture shop, so I nipped inside where he couldn't see me. I could still see him though, through the glass window.

The shopman came down on me. He had an old-fashioned suit on, collar and tie. 'Can I help you, *sir*?' he says. I didn't like the way he said *sir*.

'I'd like to buy a double bed,' I said.

'That's the way out,' he says, pointing to where I'd come in. But I could see that the furniture shop ran along the High Street for miles, it looked like. Steven was still outside, looking in at a window full of stuffed sofas.

When I'm rich I'll buy a stuffed sofa and put my muddy boots up on it.

I pushed past the shopman, crawled on my belly behind the sofas Steven was looking at, and made for the way out higher up the street.

I looked back down the street from behind a roll of lino. Steven started to walk ahead again. But I reckoned I was far enough away to make a dash for it. He wasn't looking out for me, was he? And I knew where I was now.

I ran on to the place where the six roads meet. I ran across two zebra crossings and made the buses and cars squeal and hoot. Well, they're not *allowed* to run you over there, are they? I nipped in one side of Camden Town tube station and out the other, and ran up past the junk-shops to the bridge over the canal.

There were a few people gawping over the other side of the bridge. I ran over to join them and a big car just missed me. Its engine made no noise at all but its hooter sounded like an electric organ.

I looked over from the bridge. There was the *Rosie* lying in the lock. The lock was full and she was ready to go out into the higher bit of water but I couldn't see Big Van anywhere.

Then I thought, *that car!* The silent motor and the hooter like an organ. It must be Eugene's Rolls. Steven had said about Eugene waiting at the Lock.

I nipped down off the bridge on to the tow-path. Past some notices – probably they said THIS WAY or KEEP OUT or something, and up to the lock.

I didn't know what to do next. I was standing between the *Rosie* and the windows of the caf which is just by the lock there. Then I saw Big Van sitting at a table tucking in to some nosh. I was just going to tap on the window to ask him what he was doing, eating without me, when I saw a bloke moving towards another table.

I didn't recognize him at first. He was wearing a zip jacket and tee shirt. Then I saw it was Eugene, the driver of the Rolls. He looked pretty different out of his posh cap and uniform. Not just part of the car.

Eugene went and sat himself at a table, right in the window and so near the *Rosie* he could almost lean out and touch her. Of course Eugene didn't know the *Rosie*. But if Steven came and sat at that table he couldn't help seeing her. And he'd be after me again.

I made myself flat against the outside of the caf so Eugene couldn't see me. But what about *Rosie*? You can't hide a canal boat.

Yes you can! I saw what I had to do.

The winding-handle was on the paddle-winder at the top end of the lock, where they'd just shut the paddles after letting the water in. I crawled along under the windows. I didn't want even Big Van to see me, he'd only argue. I snitched the winding-handle and crawled back to the bottom paddles. I reckoned they couldn't see me there, hoped not anyway. I fitted the handle on to the gear and wound like crazy. The water started running out. I nipped over the other side and opened the other one. Then I jumped on board, taking the handle with me.

The water rushed out and *Rosie* slowly sank below the level of the top of the lock. I looked out between the curtains, and I thought I saw, through the window of the caf, Steven making for the table where Eugene was sitting.

Then I couldn't see anything, only the slimy walls of the lock. But I knew they couldn't see me or the *Rosie* either.

I thought a bit, and dropped the winding handle over the side into the bottom of the lock.

It was quiet down there when the water finished running out. Only one or two little leaks piddling out of the brickwork, and some coming through under the doors in front. I felt safe enough, but I couldn't just stay there and wait for things to happen.

There was a sort of ladder of slimy iron rungs going up the side of the lock. I climbed up and looked carefully over the edge. No one seemed to be watching. I went quickly across the tow-path, crawled along, and scrunched myself up under the window where Eugene had been sitting. Maybe I'd hear something interesting.

The window was open and low voices came out to me from only a few inches away – Eugene's, Steven's and the woman's.

And they were talking about *snakes* again! I couldn't hear it all, and what I did hear didn't make much sense.

'The snakes have done us no harm. Why should we kill them?' It was the woman speaking. Well, I was glad they felt sorry for something, if it was only snakes.

'You have not understood,' it was Eugene's voice. 'The snakes are not to be killed. They are to be liberated.'

'They've done us no good either,' came Steven's voice. 'Why should we liberate them?'

'Listen,' Eugene's voice sounded a bit riled. 'For the snakes – we don't care about them. But think – so many snakes, free in the middle of London!'

Then they went on to talk about jelly. And I don't think it was what they had on their plates. 'It is there', says Eugene. 'In the back of the Rolls.'

'No cream this time?' says Steven. 'That was a load of trouble you brought us. The kid and the picture.'

'And they gave you the slip!' says Eugene.

'I tell you the picture is safe,' says Steven. 'As for the boy – if I set eyes on him, he will not be safe! I have my eyes open for him.'

Not all that open, I thought. And just then, round the corner comes Big Van and another bloke. They looked at the lock and their eyes popped open.

'Didn't we leave the lock full?' says Big Van to the other.

'Sure we did,' says the other bloke. 'Someone's let the water out!'

They saw me squatting under the window. 'Did you do it?' Big Van asked. I made all sorts of signs to him, pointing to the window, putting my finger to my lips, pretending I had a gun and shooting, trying to tell him the gunmen were there.

'Cheeky young nipper!' says the other bloke. 'If he's gone and let all that water out I'm going to give him a belting! I've had just about enough of these kids mucking about with my lock!' And he came along at me.

I didn't want a belting from the lock-keeper or whatever he was. But I was more scared of the gunmen. I couldn't say anything or they'd hear my voice. I made a lot more signs. They must have looked pretty wild, because the lock-keeper stopped.

'What's the matter with him? Deaf-and-dumb, or nutty? Didn't ought to be let loose!'

Big Van stood there for a bit, trying to make out what I was up to. I heard the voices from inside the caf, Eugene saying, 'Right, we'll be off then, I have the Rolls parked in Commercial Place.' Their voices seemed to move away from the window. But now they'd be coming out and I had to hide somewhere else. I nipped across the tow-path and down the slimy iron ladder to the bottom of the lock where the *Rosie* was.

'Let me get down at him!' I heard the lock-keeper say. But Big Van said, 'I'll deal with him. He's my supercargo.' I didn't like the sound of that word, but he didn't seem too mad.

'Where's the handle, you young scoundrel?' came from Big Van, peering over the edge of the lock. I pointed into the water.

I heard the lock-keeper say some bad words and then, 'I'll have to fetch the spare one.' I hoped it would take a good time. Big Van didn't say anything up there. I supposed he'd chuck me off when they got the lock open.

After a bit there was the clanking of the winding-gear and water began to sloosh in the front end. *Rosie* slowly rose. I pulled

all the window curtains together and hoped the gunmen weren't lined up on the lock-side watching.

When the window came above the edge of the lock I could see the road-bridge over the canal. And driving slowly across it was the posh grey Rolls, with three heads in it. It didn't stop.

But I stayed inside while Big Van started up the engine and steered the Rosie out of the lock. He was still not saying anything as we chugged up the next bit of canal. At least he hadn't chucked me off.

I went out to where he was steering and said, 'Sorry, Big Van, but –'

'No buts!' he cut me off. 'Either you're sorry or you're not.'

Well, I wasn't sorry. But you know, I had to say something nice. *Me, apologizing!*

'Sorry, Big Van,' I said.

'All right,' he says. He was stuffing his pipe with tobacco.

'I see you've got your shoes,' he says.

'Yes,' I said. 'Er – thanks very much.' Me saying *thank you* and all!

'Where are the matches?' he says.

That spoilt it. They were in the trolley in the supermarket. I'd have to do some explaining. But first I remembered my lighter. I lit it and helped him light his pipe. He puffed away and looked calmer.

'I was buying the matches,' I said, 'And I met these gunmen. I followed them to the lock and I heard them talking about liberating the snakes. They had jelly in the Rolls.'

'You read too many newspapers,' he says.

'That'll be the day!' I said.

'Too much telly then.' I liked that! Hadn't seen the box for *days!* 'It's all in your head,' he says.

And then a loud voice boomed across the water. 'ROSIE AHOY! THE PIRATES ARE ABOUT TO RAID YOU!'

Pirates? Well, *that* wasn't in my head!

11·PIRATES

I ran up to the front of the boat to see what was going on. Beyond a dark bridge the sun was shining on a red boat with gold decorations and two red-and-white striped sails. A whole lot of kids were mucking around it in canoes and little rowing boats.

Bang! It wasn't very loud but it made me jump. There were a couple of guns at the end of the boat and one of them had gone off! I'd been thinking quite a lot about guns just before, and I didn't like it much.

The boats and canoes were coming towards us. *Rosie* didn't have any guns, but there was a dirty great mop with a long handle, that Big Van used for swabbing decks. I grabbed it and dipped up a good lot of canal water over the side. What was it you had to do? I remembered some telly serial. *Repel boarders!*

A fat boy in a little rowing-boat was getting near the *Rosie*. 'Anything for the Pirates?' he asked. I'd give him pirates! He got a swipe over the earhole with a mop full of canal water.

He backed away with his oars. I must say he seemed to know quite a lot about rowing. About swearing too!

I looked around for more weapons. There was a bucket with a long rope on it. I let it down over the side and let it fill. It was all I could do to haul it up again.

Rosie was moving down on another rowing-boat with two quite big girls in it. They were trying to get out of the way, but they'd got their oars mixed up. One of them shouted up to me, ''ere, you're supposed to give us money!' I gave them a bucket

of slimy water over their nice long hair. Maybe they couldn't row, but they could swear all right.

I reckon these pirates weren't used to being repelled. They cleared off for a bit, but there was a lot of shouting, to each other and at me.

'Who does he think he is?'

'Toffy-nosed snob in his big boat!'

'Thinks he's being *funny*!'

'Let's *do* 'im! He started it.'

'All right mate, we're going to *get* you!'

I soaked the mop and filled up the bucket again and looked around for anything else. There were quite a lot of old paint pots with bits of different coloured paint, waiting to be chucked away. I'd chuck 'em!

The fat boy was giving orders. 'Skippers and mates lead the attack! Trusties stand by!' Some little kids were hopping up and down on the red boat shouting, 'We want to have a go!' The fat boy shouted back, 'Keep out of this, barge-mice! That's an order!'

They came at me all at once, canoes, rowing-boats, even a little flat boat with an engine in the back. I didn't think I had much of a chance but I wasn't going to give in. I kept them off with paint pots as long as I could. I got a direct hit on a canoe that spread green paint over the paddler's orange life-jacket, and he tipped over and went in. It kept some of them busy fishing him out.

I let a couple of boats have a bucket of water between them, and ran around with the mop keeping off the others. But they were all round the boat now. I shouted to Big Van for help, but when I looked round he just seemed to be killing himself laughing. There was a lot of whistle-blowing from the bank and the big loud voice shouting something. Then some sneaky lot jumped on me from behind and they were all on top of me.

'Chuck him in the water!' someone said. I lashed out with my wooden soles, but they got them off me.

The whistle-blowing was on board now, and a grownup voice

was saying, 'All right, all right, that's *enough*! Let him go!' The fat boy got off my chest and I sat up.

The grownup who'd told them to stop was saying to Big Van, 'Sorry, Mr Vandergraft! But your lad did start it.'

Big Van said to him, 'That's all right. He asked for it.' *Some pal!* He wasn't going to help me, I could see. I was still surrounded by pirates at the front end of the boat.

I said to the fat boy, 'I never started it! You came and asked for money.'

'We're *allowed* to,' says one of the wet girls.

'You're not,' I told her. 'My brother Elvis got six months for it.'

'Pirates are allowed to,' says another kid. 'We do it all the time.'

'Go on!' I said. You don't know half the rackets that go on in London!

'Them tourist boats that come along here, *Jenny Wren* and *Jason*, we get ten pee a head from them, often,' says the other wet girl.

'Oh *well*,' I said. 'Ten pee a time. That ain't mugging, that's begging. You still ain't allowed, though.'

The fat boy said, 'We *are*, then. So long as we spend it on boats and the castle.'

'What castle?' I asked.

'We're building one on the bank there,' says a boy. I looked where he was pointing, but there was nothing but a lot of broken brick walls, and weeds growing over them.

'Only we haven't started yet,' says another kid.

A castle! Funny, it was the first thing I thought of spending my million on. On the bus.

'It'll take a lot of ten pees to build a castle,' I said.

'That's what I reckon,' says the fat boy. 'But the Lord says we can do it.'

The Lord? I don't know why, I thought of Mrs Smotnik. 'You mean Him up there?' I asked, pointing to the wet clouds closing over the sky again.

They had a good giggle at that. 'No,' says one of the girls, 'Him along the canal. He's a real Lord. He done a picture of this castle and they're going to build it for us.'

Maybe I was missing out on something.

'Can I be a pirate?' I asked.

They looked at each other.

'Do we want him?' asked the fat boy.

'After what he done to us?' says one of the wet girls.

'It'd give us a chance to get even,' says the other girl.

'It'll cost you twenty-five pee to get in,' says the fat boy.

I said, 'I've got more than that. I've got –' I was going to say I'd got a million. But I shut my mouth again. They'd called me a snob in a big boat already.

I got up and went to the back of the boat where Big Van was chatting with the other bloke. I stood around for a bit waiting for them to stop talking, but they didn't. So I broke in, 'Big Van, can I speak to you, personal?'

He looked at me as if he'd forgotten about me. Then he said, 'Excuse me,' to the other bloke and we went into the kitchen together. He raised his eyebrows.

'You know that picture?' I said. 'I want to give the money for the pirates' castle.'

He looks at me over his pipe and his eyebrows go up some more.

'Fine!' he says. 'How are you going to sell it?'

You know, I'd forgotten about that. Then I had another idea.

'People pay just to *look* at pictures, don't they?' I said.

'Yes but –' he began. Then he slaps his knees again and gives a big laugh. 'We'll *do* it, by thunder! If it ruins me!'

It seems I'd started something. With the pirates' help we got the *Rosie* tied up alongside the tow-path. Big Van chose a lot of his pictures and showed us how to put them out along the racks so people could look at them. And, of course, *the* picture too.

Then he got a big board and started writing words on it. I was hopping to know what it was about, but I didn't like to say I couldn't read it. They might not let me in the Pirates if I couldn't read.

Luckily, a little girl spelt it all out as Big Van wrote it.

'Ay, ar, tee – ART,' she read. 'E, ex – EX. EX-HIB. It? I *know* – EXHIBITION! ART EXHIBITION . COME . AND . SEE . THE . Em , eye , ell , ell , eye – *Milli* ? ON . MILLION ! POUND . Pee , eye , see – PICTURE . COME AND SEE THE MILLION-POUND PICTURE!'

All the other kids laughed and jeered.

'Go on, million-pound picture!'

'No one's going to believe that one!'

'It's a rip-off, ain't it, mister?'

They crowded round the picture, which they hadn't really looked at before.

'It *is*, you know!'

'Course it ain't!'

'I saw it on the telly.'

'I saw it in the paper.'

'That's a photo.'

'That's no photo!'

'It's a copy, stands to reason.'

'It's a fake.'

'It's a rip-off!'

'Well, it ain't half like it.'

I didn't say anything, but I began to see what Big Van was up to. *Tell the truth and they don't believe you.* They asked me what it was.

'It's the million-pound picture. I nicked it,' I told them. They hooted and fell about laughing at me.

It worked! I hoped it would work with grownups.

Big Van put some more writing on the board saying it was *adults fifty pee, children ten, in aid of the Pirate Club.* We stuck it up outside the boat and put out a gangway for people to get on board. I asked Big Van if I could sit there and take the money.

He asked if I could manage. I told him not to worry. Me, I

can manage money. Letters and figures may do funny things, but coins and notes don't go wrong. You've got them in your hands.

It was a nice evening now and there were quite a few people out on the tow-path. The first to stop at our notice were two old ladies taking their little doggie for a walk.

'Fifty pence seems rather a lot, dear,' says one. 'That's ten shillings, you know.'

'It's to get those rough children off the street and into the canal, dear,' says the other.

'Oh well,' says the first. 'That *does* seem a good idea.' She asked me if their doggie could come on board and when I said he could come for nothing she gave me a pound note. They came on board and seemed to be more interested in Big Van's kitchen than the paintings.

The next was a gloomy sort of bloke who came along the tow-path muttering to himself. He stopped and read the notice.

'Million-pound picture!' he nattered. 'A likely story! As if they'd put it on show if they had it! All a fraud! Ought to be reported!'

'I'll tell you something else, mister,' I said to him. 'Them pirates ain't real pirates neither. Think yourself lucky!'

He muttered and nattered a bit more, but he counted out some silver and coppers and threw them down on my little table. He didn't stay long, and came stamping out saying he was going to report us to the police.

I didn't like it, but I thought he really wouldn't do it.

A man and a woman in trendy clothes came along holding hands, read the notice, laughed, and gave me a pound note. I heard their voices inside talking to Big Van. They seemed to want to *buy* one of his pictures, one he'd done himself!

Two-fifty in no time at all! We weren't doing bad. I looked up and down the canal for more customers. There were a couple of blokes coming along who looked like money.

The fat boy, who was sitting on the roof near me, said, 'Hey up! It's the Lord.'

I looked again. 'It's the Egg!' I said.

I thought maybe the Egg was the Lord. But when they stopped by the gang-plank it was the other one who called out to the kids on the roof, 'Hullo there, what tricks are you up to now?'

The Pirates just grinned a bit and said, 'Wotcher, Pegleg!'

The fat boy whispered in my ear, 'You ought to let him in free.' So I said, 'Free pass.' But the Lord says, 'No no, I insist,' and hands over his fifty pee like the others.

The Egg didn't put his hand in his pocket. I wasn't going to let him get away with it. 'You and all!' I said.

'I get in most galleries free,' he says, trying a nice smile. I don't think he recognized me. He'd hardly looked at me the other night.

'Mean old skinflint,' says one of the little girls perching on the roof.

'Poor old beggar,' says another. 'Hasn't drawn his pension this week.'

The Egg's neck went pretty red, or at least the bit where his neck ought to be. He pulled out his wallet and threw me a five-pound note. And he didn't stop for the change! Eight pounds! But I could only guess what would happen when he saw the exhibition, and I didn't have much time for guessing, because there on the bank was Natterer again, with a copper.

It was poor old PC Crippens again. Or poor young PC Crippens if you like. I could see he was pretty uncomfortable, tugging at the chin-strap of his helmet where it went round his beard. Natterer points out our notice to him, and he stands there spelling it out to himself.

Then they came up the gang-plank. Natterer was going to walk past me, but I said, 'Entrance fifty pee!'

'I've paid once already,' he snaps.

The copper's hand went to his pocket, as if he thought perhaps *he* ought to pay.

I said, 'Cops in uniform free.' I was enjoying this. Then I said to Natterer, 'All right mate, in you go. Didn't have much of a look, did you?'

They both went in. I wondered what to do. Maybe it was time for Ringo to make himself scarce. Nothing to stop me from pushing off with eight quid – well, nothing but a lot of pirates. But I had to know what was going on inside there.

I said to the fat boy, 'Like to take the gate, mate?' He sat down at the table and I nipped inside.

The two old ladies were sitting with their doggie in the kitchen, gawping at Big Van's racks of little jars. The trendy couple were looking through racks of Big Van's paintings. Big Van, the Egg, the Lord, Natterer and the copper were standing in front of my million-pound picture.

Natterer was waving his finger and saying, 'Let's get this straight. Either it's the real picture and this man's a thief. Or it's not the real picture and he's a fraud. Do your duty, constable!'

He was dead right, you know. Couldn't have put it clearer myself. Funny thing was, it didn't worry me. I felt he was too clever to do any harm.

PC Crippens pulls himself up as straight as he can without hitting the roof and says, 'It's all right, sir. We have the matter in hand. Sorry you've been troubled again, Sir Derrick.'

The Egg does his bending-over-the-painting bit again, all very cool again. 'Quite all right, officer,' he says. 'I was just taking my evening walk along the towpath with my friend. Mr Vandergraft, please accept my apologies for being a little hasty the other night. And let me congratulate you on this extremely competent copy. Seeing it by daylight, of course, there's no mistaking it for the real thing. The Old Masters weren't meant to be seen by electric light.'

I had to keep things straight for myself. At the police station he'd said Big Van's copy was the real picture. Now he was saying the real thing was a copy. That let us out, anyway.

Natterer turns to the copper. He cocks his thumb at the Egg and says, 'Who does he think *he* is?'

The copper says, stiff-like, 'Sir Derrick doesn't need to *think* who he is. He is Director of the Lyle Gallery. And One of Our Foremost Art Experts.'

'Then the picture's a fraud!' snaps Natterer. 'False trade description! I charge this man with obtaining money by false pretences!'

'Have we obtained any?' Big Van asked me.

'Eight pound,' I told him. 'For the Pirates' castle.'

'Better charge the Pirates!' says the Lord to the Natterer. 'And if you ask me, this copy's as good as the real thing. Can't see a ha'porth of difference myself. Worth every bit of a million, eh, Vandergraft?'

Natterer makes his eyes pop a bit, runs his fingers through his rusty hair, and stamps off without another word.

So, we were in business, or rather the Pirates were. After that it got to be quite a drag. Big Van, the Egg and the Lord and the two old ladies had coffee together. Quite a few other people came in from the tow-path and paid their fifty pee.

There was one that didn't come on board, though. I looked out from the kitchen and just saw this back view of someone running up the path away from the *Rosie*. It was getting darkish again and I couldn't see too clearly, but I thought I recognized that run.

Wasn't it Shane? Elvis's mate?

That would be just my luck! I'd dodged the Glasses gang, and they thought they had the picture safe up in Mrs Smotnik's room. We were OK with the police and the art experts and the nobs who lived along the canal. They'd all seen my picture stuck up on show, and said how kind it was of us to do it for those rough children!

The Pirates were happy with a hatful of notes and coins we'd collected at the door. Big Van was happy, he'd sold some of his own pictures. I'd have been happy with my bunk on board the *Rosie*. The only thing I was worried about was my own brother. Well, half-brother.

The Pirates went ashore, though quite a few of them didn't see why they shouldn't stay on board like me. I let go the ropes and we took in the gang-plank. We chugged on up the canal to look for a berth for the night.

It came on to rain in buckets. It was fair sizzling down into the water in the light of our headlamps. We passed under bridges and saw the people hurrying home under umbrellas. I bet they wished they could have a snug home they could take with them, like the *Rosie*.

On one bridge there's a bloke standing in the rain, without a raincoat or umbrella, looking like he's going to jump in and end it all.

There's a fair amount of light coming down from the street lamps, and the rain twinkling down all golden. The face of the bloke on the bridge was in the dark, though. But as we went under the bridge, his body suddenly stiffened, like he'd seen something.

I went stiff too. I'd seen something.

It was Elvis.

12·JUNGLE

I ducked down quick into the cabin. I tried to tell myself, *maybe Elvis hadn't seen me. Maybe I hadn't even seen Elvis.* But, you know, when two people see each other, there's no mistaking it.

The cosy-*Rosie* feeling was all gone. I felt I was on the run again. I mean, I could *explain* it all to Elvis. The buses, the angels, the Glasses gang, Mrs Smotnik, the drain-pipe, the coppers, the pirates . . .

It'd take a bit of time though. And meanwhile? He might do something nasty to me.

He'd be mad at me all right. How long was it since I got the picture? One night in the underground. Two nights in the *Rosie*. Could it be only three days ago? All the same, long enough for him to think all sorts of things about me.

Still, we were on the move, chugging through the dark. It's not so easy to catch up with a canal boat, even though they don't go very fast. With any luck we'd disappear down another tunnel, then I'd be safe. One piece of luck, there didn't seem to be any steps down from that bridge to the tow-path.

Chugger, chugger, chugger. 'Can't we go a bit faster, Big Van?' I asked him. I didn't feel I could tell him why I wanted to.

'She's doing her best,' he says. 'I'd like to make Little Venice for the night.' That sounded all right. Little Venice sounded like another country.

'Any more locks?' I asked. Another lock, and I'd be sunk!

'No locks,' he says. 'A longish tunnel though.' Just the job! I felt better.

Chugger, chugger, chug, chug – cough! Big Van looked a bit worried. I was worried too. If the engine was going to conk out on us!

Chug, chug – cough! Splutter – chug, chug. Stop . . .

It had died on us. One short sharp word from Big Van, then he steered the boat into a bank where there wasn't a tow-path.

'I suppose we can spend the night here,' he mutters to himself. 'Out you get and tie us up!'

I tied up to some railings, and got wet doing it. I looked up and down the canal. No tow-path this side, nobody about the other side. No roads near, nor houses even. Trees in the lamp-light. It seemed pretty quiet. I'd no idea where we were.

I'd have felt safer in Camden High Street. I got back into the boat and asked Big Van, 'Can't you mend the motor?' He said maybe he could, but he'd wait till daylight.

I don't remember what Big Van cooked for supper that night. I reckon I ate it all right, I must have been hungry after all those locks and all, but I kept listening and looking out of the win-dows. There was only the rain beating on the roof and pelting into the canal. And, far off, a roar like I used to hear when I stayed near the sea once. Only here it was the traffic of course.

Big Van was happy enough. He wanted to chuckle over the way the Egg and the coppers had got themselves all tied up in knots about the picture and the copy. But he soon got fed up with me not listening to him, and he said if I was that tired I'd better go to bed.

I didn't want to go off all the way to the other end of the boat by myself. But after we'd washed up he said he was sleepy too. 'I'm going to turn in,' he says.

He locked the doors, but that didn't make me feel much safer. I didn't see the locks or window-catches stopping Elvis, not if he meant to get at me in the night.

I could see Big Van's light shining out of his window on to the bank. Then it went out. I got up, went into where the pictures were, took my picture and put it in a black plastic bag, and took it to my bunk with me. I meant to hang on to it, whatever happened.

I didn't see why Elvis should have it now. He'd only nicked it from the big house. It had taken him a couple of minutes. Who had saved it from the washing machine? from the angels? from the coppers? from the Glasses gang? Who'd had it hanging from the back of his pants over the canal? Me.

You know, if someone had held out a million one-pound notes for it then, I'd have been sorry to see it go. I'd got sort of *attached* to it.

I tried not to go to sleep. I turned off my light, maybe they'd miss us in the dark. I sat up, listening.

Funny, the things you think you hear when you listen in the night! There was a good bit of wind, as well as the rain. The wind was doing wind-things in the trees over the canal. There was the traffic noise, and a train rattling along and hooting. But then I started hearing noises I couldn't put a name to. Not town-noises. Not dog-noises or cat-noises. I don't know how to tell about them.

Maybe I did doze off for a bit. But suddenly I was wide awake, listening to some new noises.

Clunk, clunk. Splash, splish. A boat, out there on the water! And it wasn't there for fun.

I tried to see out of the window. Street-lamps, some way off, shining on the water. Nothing moving that I could see. But the sounds came again, from somewhere back by the bridge. I couldn't just sit there and wait for whatever was coming.

I opened one of the windows, climbed through on to the deck outside, and pulled the picture through after me. I looked down the canal. Coming away from the shadow of the bridge I could see a long dark shape with curly ends. It was like the old canoes the Red Indians have. Who was playing Indians at this time of night?

Whoever they were, they weren't very good at it. The strong wind was blowing them down the canal, away from the *Rosie*. The clunking and splashing was the bloke trying to keep the canoe straight against the wind. There seemed to be two people in the canoe, but only the one with a paddle.

I could have nipped off on to the bank then, but I had to be sure who it was. The canoe came up slowly against the wind. I could see the face of the bloke with the paddle. It was Shane.

He saw me. 'That you, Ringo boy?' he said. 'We're coming for you.' I didn't like the way he said it.

'It's all right,' I said. 'I've got the picture for you.'

'You better had,' came Elvis's voice from the back of the canoe.

They were just about level with the back of the *Rosie*, but the wind was blowing the canoe off again.

'Reach me the end of your paddle,' I told Shane. He held out the paddle. I grabbed the end of it, put my foot against the side rail and jerked as hard and sharp as I could.

Shane just saved himself from falling in the water. But I'd got the paddle, as I'd meant to. The canoe lurched, nearly tipped over, and the wind caught it and blew it across and down the canal.

I was over the other side of the *Rosie*, on to the bank, and over the railings there, while they were still swearing and trying to get their balance. I'd got the picture with me.

They must have seen me go, but all they could do was paddle with their hands in the cold water, and try and get to the bank. I left them at it.

It was dead easy getting over the little low fence along the canal bank. But where was I now? I didn't know, I just ran on. A lane with wire-netting fences. Gardens inside, but they had no flowers or grass that I could see. Long low houses with no lights in the windows. Nobody about in the lane, no cars or anything.

And there was something really funny about this place. The *smell*! I'd noticed it on the *Rosie*, and I thought it was just the canal. But the further I ran from the canal, the worse it got. Not the usual smells of motor-cars and trucks. I couldn't think what it was. But, d'you know, it made the hairs at the back of my neck prickle?

I ran along the lane and turned up a slope. There were only a few little lights about but I could see where it led to. A tunnel. *Another tunnel!* It didn't seem to be a canal tunnel, nor yet a railway tunnel or a road tunnel. I supposed it was a people tunnel, and I made for it. I'm not that fond of tunnels, but it looked like a place to hide. And to get out of the rain.

I ran into the dark there and stopped and listened. Wind and rain. Traffic noises still a long way off. No! All of a sudden a car seemed to go by, right overhead. But I could see nothing.

I listened some more. Those noises I thought I heard from the canal – I thought I heard them again. Noises like nothing I'd heard before, yet I thought they came from something alive. Now they seemed to come from all round me. Not very loud. Not very often. But it was like I was surrounded by strange things in the dark, calling to one another.

I stood there, sort of frozen. I'd got pretty wet in the rain. My eyes were getting used to the dark, and I could see strange things on the roof of the tunnel. No writing, just animals with long horns and long legs.

If only I knew where I was! Or wasn't I really anywhere? Maybe I'd dozed off on the *Rosie* and I was dreaming all this.

When you dream, sometimes you know you're dreaming. But you never really think you're dreaming when you're awake. I was awake all right. I clung on to the only thing I had. The picture in the black plastic bag.

Voices from the other end of the tunnel!

At first I was glad there was someone alive in this rotten place. Then I thought maybe it was Elvis and Shane, waiting for me. Though I didn't see how they could have got there before me.

Bits of whisper came back along the tunnel to me.

'. . . liberty for the snakes! . . .'

'. . . if it kills them! . . .'

'. . . reptiles an'all . . .'

'. . . pythons in the park . . .'

'. . . crocodiles in the canal . . .'

'... cobras in the cafes ...'

'... rattlesnakes in the prams ...'

I knew those voices. It was Steven and the woman. *But what did it all mean?*

Best for me to get clear of them anyway. I moved quietly away to my end of the tunnel.

Voices at that end too!

Bits of whisper came back to me.

'... crooked little snake! ...'

'... dirty little toad! ...'

'... yellow little rat ...'

'... making monkeys out of us ...'

'... thinks he'll get away with it ...'

I knew those voices too. And what they meant and all. It was Shane and Elvis, after me.

Five of us, sheltering from the rain in the tunnel. And me trapped in the middle. I huddled up as best I could in the shadows. I could hear the whispers from both ends, but I suppose they couldn't hear each other.

I heard Shane say, 'Come on, he may have gone through this tunnel.'

I heard the woman say, 'Come on, we can't stay here all night.'

I crouched right down behind my black picture. It was all I could do. Down on the floor there, my fingers met something small and hard. Like a little key.

All I wanted was a little door to disappear through!

Footsteps from Steven and the woman's end. And they were going away! I crept quietly up the way they were going. At the end of the tunnel there were thick bushes. I crept right into them, into darker darkness. Footsteps from Shane and Elvis's end came along the tunnel towards me. I heard Shane say, 'Shh! There's someone ahead!'

Their quiet footsteps passed by me. They were near enough to touch, but they didn't stop. They went on after Steven and the woman.

Let them sort each other out! All I wanted was to get out of this place, wherever it was.

Should I turn back to the *Rosie*? No, they'd find me there again. I let their footsteps die away, crept out of the bushes and went off in the same direction. There had to be a way out somewhere.

There was a turning off, and I took it. More long low buildings, like a bus station. Notices that I could see in the lamplight. *If only I could read them, I'd know where I was.*

Rain was still pouring down. I slipped into a sort of bus shelter. I peered about, trying to see, and I felt around with my hands. A big glass window, so it must be a kind of shop. A door, shut. A keyhole. And I had the little key in my hand still. No reason why it should fit, but I'll try anything. I pushed the key in the keyhole and turned it.

At that moment I saw the face in the window.

I went dead cold all over and couldn't move a finger. That face! I don't know how to tell about it. He was black. Great big squidgy nose, black wrinkly mouth, black eyes looking straight at me, black eyebrows scowling at me. A great black mountain of hair on his head. His head alone was as big as me. And the body – well that was all in dark shadow and I couldn't see the end of it.

Only a bit of glass between him and me. And I'd turned the key in the lock.

I have to be dreaming all this, I told myself. *It's the way dreams go.* Because what happened next didn't make sense either.

I seemed to hear a loud voice – a posh voice rather like a teacher I once had. I can't remember what it said, but it went on and on like a teacher about the jungles of Africa. And it seemed to be coming, not from the Face, but from the keyhole.

My legs came back to me and I ran. No use trying to keep quiet with that voice booming away. And I nearly ran slap into –

A bloke taking his doggie for a walk?

Oh, *no!* This made sense all right. A security man with a guard dog.

You know, I was almost glad to see him. But he let out a bellow and I turned back and ran off the other way.

I didn't know where to run to, except away from the man and the dog. And the place wasn't like a real town with streets and pavements. It seemed to go on and on, lanes and fences, strange tall buildings, long low buildings. That smell all the time. And the noises I'd been hearing, they seemed to get louder, coming from the buildings as I ran past them. High noises and low noises, and stampings and rufflings.

I jumped over a little low fence on to some grass. Ran a few steps, tripped over something, and came down crash.

I heard the security man shouting, 'Stop there, or I'll let the dog on you!' This was it. I'd never get away from that dog.

I heard footsteps running away. Then the footsteps of the guard and the choked breathing of the dog going away after them. The man and the dog must be after Steven and the woman, or Shane or Elvis.

I lay panting there, and I looked back to see what I'd tripped over. It was a low smooth rock, a bit higher than my knees.

And as I looked at the rock, it grew a head and legs, and started to walk away, very slow.

Well, I didn't care whether it was a dream or not a dream now. Either way, *I had to find out what it all meant.*

I looked across the grass to a building with big letters on it like a shop front. I got up and stepped over the little fence again. There was a little label on it. I walked across to a building. It had a notice with lots of little words on it. Words and words and words and words, everywhere I looked. They all seemed to want to tell me something. *Let me read, just one little word!*

Me, wandering round this place in the middle of the night, trying to *read!*

There was one little word, that seemed to come everywhere. On the big shop front, among the little words on the notices, stuck on to the beginning of long words.

Two wheels. All right, I know, two o's. Oh, oh!

The zigzag. The buzz letter. Zzzzzzz.

Oh, oh, zzzz? Oze?

Ozo?

Zzzz, oh, oh? Zowo?

Zoe? Zaw? Zoo?

ZOO!

It came out and hit me between the eyes. That was what all the notices were trying to tell me! *The* zoo! The place in London where they keep all the animals!

The smell! The noises! The face! The walking rock! The talking keyhole! That one little word had made *sense* of it all. And I'd read it for myself.

I'd never *been* to the zoo. My class at school had been, not long ago. If I'd known they were going I'd have gone to school that day. But that little word, *zoo*, reminded me of everything my mates had told me. Smelly animals in cages. Screaming birds. Great apes and tortoises. And talking machines to tell you all about it.

I was really glad that little word had told me it wasn't a bad dream!

13·BLAST

Well, if I could get into the Zoo that easy, I ought to be able to get out again. On one of the notices was something I reckoned was a map. You know, one of the things people look at when they want to go somewhere. They never made much sense to me. I didn't try to push my luck by reading that. One word a night, that's good going for me!

Besides, there was something that still didn't make sense to me. All right, this was the Zoo. But what was the Glasses gang doing here? *And what was this about liberating snakes?*

Why didn't I just get the hell out of it? But me, I'm dead curious. I had to make sense of this bit.

The grumblings and squawkings of the animals and birds seemed to be coming from back where I'd started. That was where it was happening. Whatever it was.

I went back past the lines of cages, keeping to the shadows as much as I could. It seemed crazy that I hadn't known they were cages before. It wasn't a dream-place any more. Just the Zoo.

There was the place I'd thought was a bus-shelter. It must have been a big monkey, gorilla or something, I'd seen behind the glass. It was bad enough, knowing that. I kept well clear of it this time.

Up against the sky I could see the sort of mountain they've got there. You can see goats and things on it, from outside in the road, without paying. But even these they'd put to bed some-where I suppose. I reckoned if I got up there I might see what was going on, so I made for it. That smell was stronger than ever there. I reckoned, too, that dog couldn't smell me out there. They really ponged, those rocks.

There was a big dark square building near the mountain. No outside cages to it. A big entrance, with letters cut into the stone. I tried to read the word, but it was too long.

PERLITES?

TRIPESEL?

PERTLIES?

It wouldn't make sense. Never mind, you can't win 'em all.

Voices from the shadows by the building. Whispers. I ducked down behind a wall at the bottom of some steps, and listened.

'What's it matter who the guard's after? He's not after us.' It was Steven.

'Well then. Set your clock.' It was the woman.

'Are you sure it's the right place?'

'It's the place. You do your job, and there'll be more snakes free in London than there are people!'

I got that prickly feeling in my back hair again. I still couldn't make out what they were up to. But this must be where the snakes were kept – and I didn't like the talk about letting them out!

Steven was speaking again. 'You don't mind if we kill a few of them?'

'There'll be only a few dead tortoises if you do it right,' says the woman.

I don't know why, but that got me riled. *These little old tortoises, I bet they'd done her no harm!*

Running footsteps again!

'They're coming this way!' Steven's voice sounded panicky.

'Have you set the clock?' says the woman.

'I can't see too well,' says Steven.

'We'll lead them off and come back,' says the woman. They ran. I peeped over the wall. It was Shane and Elvis coming after them. But why?

Then I saw why. After Shane and Elvis came the guard and the dog, the man breathing hard and the dog near choking on his collar.

The man was shouting, between puffs, 'Stop! . . . You're trespassing! . . . enclosed premises!'

Trespassing! There was something worse than that going on here, if he only knew. But what was it? I came out from behind the wall and crossed the pathway to where Steven and the woman had been crouching. It was shadowy, but I could make out a bag tucked behind a drain-pipe. It seemed to be a black dust-bin bag, like the one I'd got under my arm. Yes, I'd still got *that* with me all right.

It makes me shiver right now, to think I opened that other bag. I couldn't see much in the dark, but there seemed to be wires and things. *And a clock ticking.*

I don't know what I thought I was going to do with it. I didn't have time to think. The running feet suddenly got nearer again – they must have run right round the building and back here again. They were round the corner and on to me before I could get out of the way.

I jumped up but somebody cannoned right into me. We both came down. It was Steven. Another body tripped over the two of us. It felt like the woman. Two more lots of running feet came round the corner and by now there wasn't room to get past. Shane and Elvis were down on top of us. And we were all still rolling around there when the boots of the guard and the snarling, panting dog were on us too.

I had one thought in my mind. *Grab the picture and get out of here!* I wriggled out from the wrestling, swearing pile, grabbed the black plastic bag, and ran off.

I ran back through that tunnel again, then instead of going down to the canal I found myself on the bridge over it. And I stopped there. Why? Well, I was holding this black plastic bag by the neck, the same as I'd been doing all the time. But it had suddenly got a lot heavier!

The moon broke through the clouds and I looked at the bag.

Wrong shape too. I opened the top and tried to look inside. There was a smell of cake. I listened.

It ticked.

I lifted it over the edge of the bridge and let it drop into the water.

There was a splash, and I could see the silvery rings it made in the moonlight. On the edge of the rings, I could see the Rosie.

There was a flash that made all the water glow green.

A thump of thunder from under the water.

A spout of hard spray that hit under the bridge like a hammer, then went on up to the moon. The bridge shook, then the water was falling back like a waterfall. I was drenched in cold water. I didn't know if the bridge was in the canal or the canal was bursting over the bridge.

The water knocked me down and I was flopping like a fish, among a stink of canal mud. And every animal in the Zoo seemed to be roaring, howling, barking, hooting, screaming, squawking.

What about the Rosie? As soon as I could think, that was what I thought. I found I could move all right. I got up and ran squelching back along the bridge and down the slope to the canal.

I could see the back end of the Rosie in the moonlight. It was only just above the level of the water. I ran to the front and jumped on board. I hollered, 'Big Van!'

I thought I heard him blundering about inside. I called out, 'Come out! She's sinking!'

I went down the steps, and my feet went into cold water. There was someone sloshing around in the picture room. I went through, with the water up to my knees, and made out Big Van. I grabbed him and hauled him towards the steps. 'It was a bomb!' I shouted. I think he'd been knocked pretty silly by the blast.

The water was gurgling in fast, and the air was making horrible wheezing, bubbling noises as it came out of the hollow bits. I dragged Big Van by the collar up the steps and over on to the bank. *Rosie* sank in swirls of water as we stepped off.

Big Van sat down on the pathway with his head in his hands. 'My pictures!' he groaned.

Well, I was more sorry for the *Rosie* than for his pictures. And what about *my* picture? It was somewhere up there, among all that noise!

On top of the voices of all the excited animals there were men shouting, whistles blowing, motors revving, and:

> beep-bawp beep-bawp *beep-bawp beep-bawp* BEEP-BAWP
> BEEP-BAWP
> BEEP-beep BAWP-bawp beepBAWP*beep bawp*BEEPbawp

There seemed to be hundreds of them already, coming from all parts of London!

They didn't take long to find us. No, not my friend PC Crippens this time. A tough-looking squad of cops. With guns. They look funny with guns, though, London coppers. You know, they didn't actually *point* them at us.

Big Van started on about how his boat had been sunk, but they didn't want to listen. They marched us up to where a lot of lights were blazing. Back along that tunnel again. That was all lit up now, and I could see the funny paintings of animals on the roof quite clear.

Well, all London was pouring into the open space at the end of the tunnel.

Coppers in helmets, coppers in caps, coppers in soft hats and mackintoshes. Panda cars and squad cars and paddywagons.

Three or four white ambulances with **AMBULANCE** on the front.

I don't know how many fire engines.

We even got the Army! A big armoured truck with a search-light on it, and soldiers in khaki jerseys.

We were marched up to a top copper. 'Put them with the others,' he says. 'We'll question them later.'

Of course the others were Steven and the woman, Shane and Elvis. We were made to stand against a wall. None of us said anything.

More revving motors. I looked round. Somebody swore and said, 'Didn't you tell those security men to keep the gates locked. Now they've let the television in!'

A cheerful voice – I reckoned I'd heard it on the box often enough – calls out, 'I hear you're waiting for another bomb.' The telly team started rigging up more lights.

I edged away from the other prisoners. Everyone seemed to be looking across the open space towards the big building, and looking worried. They didn't seem to notice me as I moved up to a bunch who were doing the talking. There was the security guard with the dog, a top copper, an Army officer, a soldier with a gun, and a bloke with white hair who seemed to have pyjamas on underneath his overcoat.

'What exactly is in that building, Professor?' the top copper was asking.

The bloke in the pyjamas said quite a lot that I didn't get. I heard some words like *peelusbungalus tinnedasprin* and *nugger-nugger* – but I may have got that wrong.

'What's that in English, sir?' asks the Army officer. He didn't seem to have got it either.

'Snakes,' says the old bloke.

'Dangerous?' asks the copper.

'I have handled them all,' says the prof. 'They're quite harmless unless they are excited or disturbed.'

'And if they get excited?' asks the copper.

'They'll bite,' says the prof. 'And I would recommend instant hospitalization.'

'But the medics could fix you up all right?' asks the Army bloke. The prof. nodded.

'But if one of us goes to defuse that bomb?' says the policeman to the Army bloke.

'There may be nothing left of him to fix!'

'We'll risk the snakes,' says the copper. The Army officer

130

turns to the soldier. 'Can you see the package?' he asks. 'Yessir,' says the soldier.

He was looking through a pair of glasses towards the black plastic bag by the drain-pipe. 'Reckon I could put a few rounds through it, sir,' he says.

Hey! *They were going to make a lot of holes in my picture!* After all the trouble I'd taken to look after it, the Army, the police and these professors and people were going to stand by and see it shot to pieces!

I didn't stop to argue. I knew I couldn't tell them the whole story. I ran across the open space towards that plastic bag.

I heard voices behind me.

'What's that boy doing?'

'Stop him!'

'Come back, you young fool!'

I ran along the side of the building, the lights behind me and my long shadow running in front. There was the black plastic bag, lying in the pathway.

I must say I did have a moment wondering if it *wasn't* another bomb. I saw myself blown sky-high, along with bits of tortoises and angry snakes. But I picked up the bag. It was the right shape and the right weight.

I took off the elastic band I'd put round the neck.

More voices from across the open space.

'Put that down, for God's sake!'

'Take cover, everyone!'

I walked slowly back in the glare of the lights. I couldn't see what the people were doing, but I was sure I heard the whirr of the telly cameras.

'Don't come any nearer with that thing!' barked a voice. 'Or we'll have to shoot!'

So I stopped where I was. I reached in the bag and pulled out the picture.

I held it up to the lights and the cameras.

14·LAST BIT

When they'd got it all sorted out they decided I was a little hero, not a villain.

It got to be quite a drag. I don't know how many times I had to tell my story about the picture and the bomb. Mostly I told it like I've told it now, but I may have got it different sometimes. They got into such a muddle about which was the real picture and which was the copy, and which was the bag with the bomb and which was the bag with the picture – well, Elvis, Shane, Steven and the woman, they all got off pretty light. Old Glasses – and I reckon he's a real nasty – sloped off somewhere and they never found him.

The million-pound picture? It's back hanging on the wall in the big old house. See for yourself if you don't believe me.

It's been a real giggle, the stories they've put in the papers. I've been cutting bits out. Yes, *me, reading newspapers!* It's different, reading, when it's about *you.*

I've had this teacher to help me, and I've started on the easy bits. The ones in big thick letters. Headlines.

Here's a few.

ZOO BLAST, BOAT SINKS
SNAKE LIB BID
ART HAUL FOUND IN ZOO
BOY FOILS BOMB GANG
BOAT BOY FOILS ART HAUL GANG'S
    SNAKE LIB ZOO BLAST BID

Well, I'm off down to the canal again. We've got something on, today. It's a sort of geratta. No, *regatta*.

We've got the *Pirate Queen*. That's the red boat with the gold decorations and red-and-white sails. And all the little rowing-boats and canoes.

We've got the *Rosie*. Oh yes, we got her bottom patched up again and I helped with scraping the muck out of her. Big Van's pictures, they mostly had to be chucked away. But he can always do some more, can't he? Actually, since he's been on telly, his old picture-factory's been so busy I've had to help him out.

And we've got the angels coming down, and all! They're going to be water-lilies or something. Still, I reckon they'll brighten up those mucky old locks no end, with all that glitter.

Come and chuck us a penny!

More books from Puffin

COME BACK SOON
Judy Gardiner

Val's family seem quite an odd bunch and their life is hectic but happy. But then Val's mother walks out on them and Val's carefree life is suddenly quite different. This is a moving but funny story.

AMY'S EYES
Richard Kennedy

When a doll changes into a man it means that anything might happen . . . and in this magical story all kinds of strange and wonderful things do happen to Amy and her sailor doll, the Captain. Together they set off on a fantastic journey on a quest for treasure more valuable than mere gold.

ASTERCOTE
Penelope Lively

Astercote village was destroyed by plague in the fourteenth century and Mair and her brother Peter find themselves caught up in a strange adventure when an ancient superstition is resurrected.

THE HOUNDS OF THE MÓRRÍGAN
Pat O'Shea

When the Great Queen Mórrigan, evil creature from the world of Irish mythology, returns to destroy the world, Pidge and Bright are the children chosen to thwart her. How they go about it makes an hilarious, moving story, full of totally original and unforgettable characters.

JUNIPER

Gene Kemp

Since her dad left Juniper and her mum have had nothing but problems and now things are just getting worse – there are even threats to put Juniper into care. Then she notices two suspicious men who seem to be following her. Who are they? Why are they interested in her? As Christmas draws nearer Juniper knows something is going to happen . . .

THE SEA IS SINGING

Rosalind Kerven

Tess lives right in the north of Scotland, in the Shetland Islands, and when she starts hearing the weird and eerie singing from the sea it is her neighbour, old Jacobina Tait, who helps her understand it. With her strange talk of whales and 'patterns' Jacobina makes Tess realize that she cannot – and must not – ignore what the singing is telling her. But how can Tess decipher the message?

RACSO AND THE RATS OF NIMH

Jane Leslie Conly

When fieldmouse Timothy Frisby rescues young Racso, the city rat, from drowning, it's the beginning of a friendship. It's also the beginning of Racso's education – and an adventure. For the two are caught up in the brave and resourceful struggle of the Rats of NIMH to save Thorn Valley, their home, from destruction.

A TASTE OF BLACKBERRIES

Doris Buchanan Smith

The moving story about a young boy who has to come to terms with the tragic death of his best friend and the guilty feeling that he could somehow have saved him.

FRYING AS USUAL
Joan Lingard

Disaster strikes the Francettis when Mr Francetti breaks his leg. Their fish and chip shop never closes, but who is going to run it now that he's in hospital and their mother is in Italy? The answer is quite simple to Toni, Rosita and Paula, and with the help of Grandpa they decide to carry on frying as usual. But it's not that easy . . .

THE FREEDOM MACHINE
Joan Lingard

Mungo dislikes Aunt Janet and to avoid staying with her he decides to hit the open road and look after himself, and with his bike he heads northwards bound for adventure and freedom. But he soon discovers that freedom isn't quite what he's expected, especially when his food supplies are stolen, and in the course of his journey he learns a few things about himself.

TWIN AND SUPER TWIN
Gillian Cross

Ben, David and Mitch had only meant to start the Wellington Street Gang's bonfire, not blow up all their fireworks as well. But even worse is what happens to David's arm in the process. Until, that is, they realize that this extraordinary event could be very useful in their battles with the Wellington Street Gang.

WOOF!
Allan Ahlberg

Eric is a perfectly ordinary boy. Perfectly ordinary, that is, until the night when, safely tucked up in bed, he slowly turns into a dog! Fritz Wegner's drawings superbly illustrate this funny and exciting story.

VERA PRATT AND THE FALSE MOUSTACHES
Brough Girling

There were times when Wally Pratt wished his mum was more ordinary and not the fanatic mechanic she was, but when he and his friends find themselves caught up in a real 'cops and robbers' affair, he is more than glad to have his mum, Vera, to help them.

SADDLEBOTTOM
Dick King-Smith

Hilarious adventures of a Wessex Saddleback pig whose white saddle is in the wrong place, to the chagrin of his mother.

WAR BOY
Michael Foreman

Barbed wire and barrage balloons, gas masks and Anderson shelters, loud bangs and piercing whines – the sights and sounds of war were all too familiar to a young boy growing up in the 1940s. Lowestoft, a quiet seaside town in Suffolk, was in the front line during World War II. Bombing raids, fires and trips to the air-raid shelters became almost daily events for young Michael Foreman and his friends.